ESCAPE

K. R. Alexander

Scholastic Inc.

ISBN 978-1-338-26047-2

10 9 8 7 6 5 4   22 23 24 25 26

Printed in the U.S.A.   40
First edition, June 2022

Book design by Keirsten Geise

For those seeking
a new adventure

ESCAPE YOUR TROUBLES! ESCAPE TO ADVENTURE!

It was the same tagline Cody had read a hundred times. But he still felt a thrill every time he read it. ESCAPE wasn't just a theme park. It was an Event. A Happening. It promised everything a kid could want, and more.

Want to cast magical spells in cutting-edge VR?

Done.

Fly among dragons and dinosaurs on a real live hang glider?

No problem.

Eat all the junk food you can stomach and stay up until four in the morning?

Go for it.

ESCAPE was built to cater to dreams. Whatever you wanted, whenever you wanted it—the moment you stepped foot within the park's doors, it was yours.

And the best part?

No. Adults. Allowed.

Cody would have given anything to go. He was obsessed. He'd read every article, interacted with every post, watched every behind-the-scenes video. But he knew, deep down, that he wouldn't get the chance.

ESCAPE wasn't built for kids like him.

He wasn't famous enough.

For the incredibly exclusive grand opening week, only a hundred tickets had been made available, given out one at a time with grand announcements.

For the first few months, Cody watched as every single ticket went to someone he knew. Not because they were his classmates, but because the kids were famous. Pop star, social media sensation, child actor, business-tycoon-kid famous. He had to watch as ESCAPE posted them one by one to its feed. The kids gloated and humblebragged about getting to go. *The chance of a lifetime*, they called it. Yeah—but to them, those chances came every day.

Cody had still liked the posts. Just in case.

Then, a month ago, the website had changed.

A registration form had appeared.

Along with it came a new promise: The final thirty kids chosen wouldn't be celebrities. They'd be selected by a random drawing.

Whoever wanted to register would have a chance.

Cody signed up. Of course he did. He clicked submit before even reading the fine print.

He would do anything to get out of his nowhere town. Even though he had a few friends, he still felt closed in. He knew Laura and Patrick didn't dream as big as him, didn't spend their days thinking of building their own massively popular theme park and traveling the world exploring new rides.

They were happy here.

He was not.

So for the next twenty-six days, Cody watched as, one by one, regular kids like him were picked from the draw.

Twenty-six more opportunities lost.

Every time, he felt like the walls were closing in a little bit tighter. Every time, he felt his chances of ESCAPE—both the theme park and getting out of his town—were slipping from his hands.

If only he'd known that soon, he wouldn't be trying to escape his boring routine.

Instead, he'd be trying to escape with his life.

Cody sat in the back of the classroom, staring at his phone, which was hidden behind his textbook, while his teacher droned on and on about the short stories they were reading. He'd barely had his phone off since the registration had gone live, twenty-six days ago. Which meant for the last month, he'd had to watch day after day as someone else got the opportunity he'd been dreaming for.

It was killing him.

"Cody Baxter!" his teacher called out.

Cody jerked and looked up.

"Yes, Mr. Kearns?"

Mr. Kearns wasn't like most of the teachers at Judkins Middle School. He was fresh out of grad school, for one thing, with a hipster beard and man bun, and he wore funky vests. Today, his vest was covered in a woolly mammoth print. He wasn't from around here, that was for sure.

Mr. Kearns was an outcast, like him. Of all the teachers here, Cody liked Mr. Kearns best. But he couldn't understand why someone—when Cody wanted nothing more than to get out—would *choose* to come here.

"I gotta ask," Mr. Kearns said. "Are you a wizard or something?"

Cody felt his face flush. A few of his classmates giggled, and every eye was on him.

"What? No. Why?"

Mr. Kearns grinned.

"Because your book is somehow magically glowing. I mean, that's the only probable cause, right? Because you wouldn't dream of being on your phone while I'm teaching. I know these stories are older than me, but they aren't that boring, are they? Surely *I'm* not that boring."

"What? No, sir."

Mr. Kearns laughed. "This isn't the army, cadet. Just put your phone away, okay? I'm doing a surprise pop quiz in three days that you'll probably want to be taking notes for."

Cody complied, and Mr. Kearns went back to teaching. Everyone hurriedly focused on their own notes, and the room was filled with the sound of scribbling pencils. He noticed that some of his classmates still looked over their shoulders at him. He wondered how many of them were writing notes to one another about him.

At the end of class, Mr. Kearns pulled him aside.

"So," he said, "what was so important that you felt the need to ignore me for most of the class?"

"I wasn't ignoring you!" Cody protested.

"Please," Mr. Kearns said. "I don't think I've seen anyone that focused in my class since, well . . . actually, no. That's the first time anyone's been that focused in my class. Maybe I should start choreographing dances to the stories we're reading."

"No, definitely don't. I mean, you don't need to do that." Mr. Kearns raised an eyebrow. Cody dropped his head. "I was looking at ESCAPE."

"ESCAPE? You mean that death trap they're calling a theme park?"

Cody nodded, even as he thought, *It isn't a death trap.*

Adults—even *cool* adults—never understood.

"Why do you want to go so badly?" Mr. Kearns asked. He didn't seem to be making fun of him, though. He actually seemed interested.

Cody couldn't answer right away. He didn't want to say too much, didn't want to tell his teacher that although his parents weren't mean to him, they weren't, well, *nice*. They didn't let him have any fun. Not strict in the normal "I can't eat ice cream for dinner or play video games until sunrise" way, but strict in the "no fun, ever" way. He wasn't even allowed video games, and only got dessert on Fridays. It wouldn't have been so bad if his parents didn't also fight all the time. But they did. Every night. The only time he got to escape was when he went over to his friends' houses, though he couldn't hide at Laura's or Patrick's forever.

Escape.

That's what he wanted. To escape to ESCAPE.

But of course, he'd never tell Mr. Kearns all that.

"I don't know," Cody lied. "I guess it just seems so much cooler than anything here, you know? You can do anything you dream of there. Fight pirates or adventure underwater or have superpowers. It's like . . . everything real life isn't."

"Yeah, but," Mr. Kearns said slowly, gently, "it's all just a game. I mean, it looks fun! Don't get me wrong. I'll totally be going when it's open to the public. But it's virtual reality. Made up. It isn't worth forgetting about what's right in front of you."

"There's nothing right in front of me," Cody mumbled.

Mr. Kearns sighed.

"Is everything okay at home?" he asked.

Cody shrugged. "Yeah. It's fine. Look, I gotta get to my next class. Thanks for not giving me detention."

"I don't punish dreamers," Mr. Kearns said. He put a hand on Cody's shoulder. "Just make sure to drop in on reality once in a while. And study for that quiz."

It was lunchtime, and once more, Cody was secretly on his phone, watching the official feed of ESCAPE. They posted the winners of the draw at different times every day. Probably to ensure that you were always watching the feed, rather than just tuning in at certain times. The last post was a sneak peek of their haunted house: a five-second video clip of some unknown kid running and screaming while a dozen ghosts and ghouls swarmed around him, the halls dripping green and breathing in and out.

Cody had watched it, like, a dozen times, trying to see how they did it. The ghosts looked so real. But he couldn't see any wires or mirrors, and it wasn't VR. He had no clue. And that was just one more reason why he wanted to go so badly. At ESCAPE, they were doing the impossible. Someday, he wanted to build his own theme park. What better way to learn than to attend the most cutting-edge park in the world?

He played the video again and tried to zoom in.

"I heard you got called out in Kearns's class," Patrick said.

Cody jumped and looked up as his friend sat down beside him.

"Yeah," Laura replied, sitting down on the other side. "What did you do? Make fun of his vest or something?"

"No," Cody admitted. "I was, you know . . ." He held up his phone.

Laura rolled her eyes, but Patrick was on board. He was also trying to win a chance to go.

"Did they announce anything yet?" Patrick asked, grabbing Cody's phone. "The last kid was revealed at nine forty yesterday morning, so I would have thought . . ."

Cody shook his head. "No, nothing yet. I keep checking, but they haven't updated."

"I still don't see why you're so obsessed with this," Laura said. "It's just a theme park. Once the grand opening is over, we can all just go together."

Both Cody and Patrick looked at her.

"With what money?" Patrick asked before Cody could say anything. "Tickets are bound to be hundreds of dollars a day, and it's like a five-hour drive. Not only does the grand opening raffle cover entry and travel, but you'd have the park basically to yourself! No lines, no wait. Plus, you'd be around all the coolest kids in the *world*."

Laura rolled her eyes again. She did that a lot when they were discussing ESCAPE. "Just because they're celebrities doesn't mean they're interesting," she said. "Honestly, I bet they're all really boring and stuck up. You couldn't pay me to spend a week surrounded by *influencers*."

"Look, we don't crush your dreams about being a bestselling YA novelist. Don't crush ours," Cody said. "You know this would be big for us. If we want to design rides—"

"I know, I know," Laura said. "This would be the opportunity of a lifetime and being part of the first group of kids means you might even land on the radar of the designers. Go from beta testers to builders. You've told me a million times." Her voice softened. "I just don't want you to get disappointed when—"

"It's updated!" Patrick yelped.

"What? Who is it?"

He held up the phone so Cody—who had crammed in super close to him—could see.

The video post—like all the announcements for the non-famous kids—was a plain white screen with text that faded in and out.

FOUR DAYS TO ESCAPE . . .

FOUR SPOTS LEFT . . .

"Come on, get on with it," Patrick grumbled. Cody couldn't speak. He couldn't breathe.

OUR 97th GUEST WILL BE . . .

"Ugh, this is so melodramatic," Laura said. But she didn't look away, either.

CODY . . .

"No way. No way no way no way," Patrick breathed beside him.

JACOBSEN.
CONGRATULATIONS!

Patrick groaned and leaned back, setting the phone on the table in disappointment.

Cody felt like he'd been punched in the gut.

He'd been so close. So close. *Why couldn't they have said my name?* Now some other Cody was going to get to go. What was the chance they'd pick another Cody to go after that?

"See?" Laura said softly. "So much anticipation and so much disappointment."

"Not now," Cody whispered. He pressed his hands to his eyes. He wasn't crying. He was just trying to blot out the world. "Please."

Laura didn't say anything.

"There's still a chance," Patrick said. He put a hand on Cody's shoulder.

But Cody knew there wasn't. There wasn't.

Cody went straight to his bedroom when he got home
from school, grabbing a sandwich on his way up. His
parents weren't really the "sit-down meal together"
sort, and he didn't want to have to interact with them
if he could help it.

He didn't want to interact with anyone right then.

The trouble was, being in his room didn't help.
At all.

Every single space on his walls was filled with
posters and drawings and diagrams. Not of bands or
cars or trains or spaceships. Of rides.

There was the drawing of the first roller coaster
he ever designed, eight years ago. He was four, and
it was in crayon, and it didn't even really look like
a roller coaster—just a bunch of blue and red lines,

really—but he'd stolen it from his parents' memory book and hung it on his wall as a reminder of his life's passion.

From there, his skill at drawing and design had gotten a *lot* better.

On that wall was a mock-up of a haunted house ride, complete with diagrams of every jump scare, every strobe placement, every mechanical ghoul. He'd even written out the *moods* of every room, the temperature changes, the slight breezes so it felt like you were being followed.

And there! His take on bumper cars. Only in these, you weren't driving your car—you were remote-controlling someone else's, and someone was controlling yours, so no one would know what was going on.

There weren't just drawings, either. He'd constructed models of attractions from clay, dioramas of entire theme parks from cardboard and Popsicle sticks. One had even won him the science fair last year, since his focus was on physics and motion. There was a LEGO roller coaster spiraling around the ceiling over his bed. That had been a gift from his parents years ago. Before they started fighting. That had been the best birthday ever. Probably because it was the last good one he ever had. It had amped up his desire to design and build rides—and reinfornced his newfound need to get as far away from here as he could.

He spun slowly on the spot.

Normally, this room made him feel good. Seeing all the drawings and designs inspired him, gave him purpose, gave him hope. But ever since ESCAPE started announcing its winners, the room had made him feel worse and worse.

It was a reminder of the life he'd probably never live.

A part of him wanted to tear it all down. Find a new hobby, something normal. Like basketball or soccer or even band. But every time he thought about changing hobbies—no, *obsessions*—he felt hollow inside. Wrong. Theme parks were just *it*.

"I'm going to get out of here," he whispered to himself and his drawings. "This is my calling."

His words made him feel better. Just for a moment. Then he heard the door open downstairs and one of his parents get home. He sighed, went over to his computer, put on his headphones, and started blaring his music.

He didn't know when his parents started fighting, only that eventually they both got home and did.

They didn't stop when he finished his homework.

They didn't stop when he brushed his teeth and got ready for bed.

They didn't stop when he turned off the lights and tried to sleep, headphones still on.

It was okay.

He was going to get out of here.

And he was never coming back.

Cody checked his phone the moment he opened his eyes.

Within seconds, still bleary eyed, he had pulled up ESCAPE's feed.

Nothing. Not even a teaser video.

Just the last update, playing on loop, announcing that another Cody was going to be living out his dream.

Downstairs, he heard his parents arguing over breakfast. Frustration grew inside him; he wanted to throw his phone out the window.

But he didn't. Of course he didn't. His phone was his lifeline. Besides, this wasn't the first morning he'd skipped breakfast because he couldn't stand to be in the same room as his parents. And, unless he got to ESCAPE, it probably wouldn't be his last, either.

He slowly got ready for school and made his way downstairs. Their arguing went silent when he walked past the kitchen toward the front door.

"Where do you think you're going without breakfast?" his mom called out.

"Did you do your homework?" his dad demanded.

Seriously, the only time they stopped fighting was when they were ganging up on him.

"Yes, Dad," he said. "I did it last night. And I'll pick something up from the gas station on the way—"

"You will not," his mom interrupted. "We don't have the money for you to be wasting it on junk food. You're going to have a real breakfast—now sit down."

"I'm going to be late," he said. "I've got to study with Patrick for a quiz before class."

That was a lie. But it was also the only way to get out of an awkward breakfast.

He didn't wait for them to say it was okay. He walked to the front door. Behind him, he heard his dad say, "You're too soft on him," while his mother countered, "Me? You're the one who refuses to give him structure."

He was out the door and down the street as fast as he could go.

He wasn't selected that day, or the next day, either.

He found out halfway through recess that someone named Jade Goldsmith was going to have their dreams come true.

"There's still a chance," Patrick told him.

But was there? Really?

There was only one spot left. What were the chances it would go to him?

Cody couldn't even respond. He just stared at the announcement on his phone and felt his heart sink slowly into his feet.

"Come on," Laura said. "Let's go, I don't know, play a game or something. You two are starting to depress me."

He let her drag him over to the basketball court,

where they shot hoops (or, really, he *tried* to shoot hoops and just ended up throwing the ball wide). He was so numb he didn't even hear the bell ring for the end of recess.

He was so numb, he didn't hear anything for the rest of the day.

Which was probably a good thing, because his parents were on a roll when he got home that night.

He locked himself in his bedroom.

When he finally fell asleep, staring at his phone screen and hoping for an update that would change his life, he couldn't even remember if he'd eaten dinner.

"Anything?" Patrick asked when Cody got to school the next morning.

"No," Cody said. "You?"

Patrick shook his head.

They'd both signed up for the raffle. And they both assumed that the winners would get some sort of notification before it went live on social media . . . but they weren't sure of that, either. The winners were entirely hush-hush about the process. Even getting in was as secretive as the place itself.

"Still time," Cody pointed out. "They haven't announced yet."

"Totally," Patrick replied. He hesitated, looking at his feet. "What are you going to do if, you know . . ."

"What?"

"If you don't get in," Patrick finished in a rush. He looked sheepishly to Cody. "I mean, I'm sure some of those celebs are going to livestream that whole week. Are you going to watch or . . . ?"

Cody hadn't given it much thought.

Well, actually, he'd given it a *lot* of thought, and he didn't want to be thinking about it at all.

If he didn't get in.

If he didn't get in, what would he do?

He'd spent the last three and a half months dreaming of himself there. Dreaming of everything the opportunity would change. It had never just been about getting to be there first, or doing something exclusive. It had been the opportunity to be around people doing amazing things. So amazing that they'd inspire him, or take him along for the ride. To be in a place where even his wildest dreams were a reality—which meant he could find ways to make his dreams a reality in the real world, too. It had been about taking a thousand steps toward his goal of creating his own theme park.

If he didn't get in, if all that was taken away from him . . .

"I don't know," he said. "I'll probably tune in, I guess."

It would kill him to see other people having fun there. It would kill him more to miss out. At least if he was watching a stream, it would sort of feel like he was experiencing it all there with them. Right?

"I mean, maybe Laura was right," Patrick ventured. "We're really getting our hopes up and I'm sure a billion kids registered. It was *international*, man. We can always pick a weekend and go ourselves. Save up some money. I've been mowing lawns and Laura has been babysitting her little cousin. It won't be the end of the world."

Cody looked down.

Okay, so maybe he wasn't being totally honest.

This *was* about being the first there. It was about feeling special and important, about being around special and important people. He'd always been passed over, always been the quiet nerdy kid most people ignored. He wanted to feel . . . well, he wanted to feel like he was *something*. And going to the park after everyone else had had their fun—it didn't feel the same. He'd still get to see the rides, sure. But that magic wouldn't be there.

"Maybe you're right," Cody admitted. *Maybe it's time to start accepting reality.*

Depression set in . . . but before it could get very far, the school bell rang, and Cody and the rest of his classmates shuffled inside.

His phone buzzed in Mr. Kearns's class.

Right in the middle of the quiz. Of course it was in the middle of the quiz.

He'd set his notifications so his email was a special pattern.

And this was definitely an email.

The only email account he had linked to his phone was the one he'd created specifically for updates from the ESCAPE raffle.

He had only gotten one email from them, and that was just after he'd signed up, as confirmation.

His hand went to his pocket, but he froze before he pulled out the phone. Mr. Kearns was looking right at him. He didn't want to push it.

He pretended to scratch his leg and went back

to answering the quiz. But he couldn't focus.

His phone buzzed again with another notification.

Two emails in a row? That can't be right.

His hand twitched, but he didn't reach for his phone. He swore everyone in the class was side-eyeing him, especially Mr. Kearns, could swear they'd all heard the vibration and were just waiting for him to slip up.

He looked up at the clock on the wall. Only ten minutes until class was over. He could check it in the hall. It would be fine. It would be fine.

His phone buzzed again.

Three emails?

He couldn't help it. Trying to be as sly as possible, he leaned back and slipped his phone partway from his pocket, just enough to see the notifications screen.

Three notifications.

Three emails.

All from ESCAPE.

But his privacy settings meant he couldn't read them until logging in.

His hand trembled. He looked up at Mr. Kearns. Thankfully his teacher wasn't looking at him.

If he was quick . . .

He pulled his phone out the whole way and entered his passcode.

The screen unlocked.

URGENT! read one.

OPEN IMMEDIATELY! read the next.

THIS IS NOT A TEST! read the final one.

He couldn't breathe. He couldn't move. *This can't be real. This can't be happening.*

He had to know what they said.

Just as he was about to open a message, his phone buzzed with a fourth email. **ANNOUNCING OUR NEWEST WINNER . . .**

"Cody Baxter!" Mr. Kearns called out.

Cody jolted in his seat. His phone skidded across the floor facedown. His brain wasn't computing. Had he just won?

He scrambled to pick up the phone, but Mr. Kearns was standing at his side, and was much faster. Mr. Kearns grabbed the phone and slipped it in his pocket. Without even looking at the screen.

"I'll be keeping this," Mr. Kearns said. He looked at Cody with real disappointment in his eyes. If Cody wasn't so nervous and excited, he would have felt bad.

"Please," Cody said. He tried to keep his voice down, but he was acutely aware that everyone in the class had given up on focusing on their quiz, and was staring at him. "Can I have it back?"

Mr. Kearns laughed. "I'm actually kind of shocked you'd ask that. You know phones aren't allowed in the classroom."

"I know, but . . ." He looked around. Whispered his next words. "I think I won."

"Judging by your quiz, I'd have to beg to differ," Mr. Kearns said. He tapped the quiz with a finger. "Finish this. If you don't get at least a B, you'll have detention for the week. And you'll get your phone back at the end of the day—"

"But!"

"Ask again, and you won't get it back at all."

"But you don't understand, I think I won! I think I'm going to ESCAPE."

Mr. Kearns sighed. "Fine. I'm keeping your phone. And I'm going to have a little chat with your parents."

Cody opened his mouth to protest, but Mr. Kearns was faster. "Don't make this worse for yourself, Cody," he said.

Cody didn't say anything.

Mr. Kearns nodded. He looked at the rest of the class. "Well? I don't see any moving pencils."

Everyone went back to work. Cody just stared at Mr. Kearns's retreating back.

Don't make this worse for yourself, he'd said. How could it get worse than this?

"I can't believe you got Mr. *Kearns* mad at you," Patrick said, almost in awe. "He's, like, a pacifist or something." They were walking down the hall between classes, and Patrick and Laura had rushed up to him—apparently, everyone in school was talking about it.

Laura huffed beside him. "I can't believe you did that in class. What were you thinking?"

"I think I got a ticket," Cody admitted.

"WHAT?!" Patrick roared.

People stopped and stared. Laura actually jumped.

"I mean, are you serious?" Patrick asked, only a little quieter.

"Yeah," Cody said. He looked at Laura. His next words were defensive. "I wouldn't have checked my phone otherwise."

"You gotta get it back!" Patrick said. "I've heard the links expire after a few hours. You know, in case they accidentally pick a bot or something."

"I can't," Cody said. "There's no way Mr. Kearns will give it back. And he's . . . he's calling my parents."

"Ugh," Laura grunted. She hated his parents.

"Wait, what if you use my phone?" Patrick suggested, completely ignoring Cody's familial plight. He pulled out his phone. "You can log in to your email and check from here."

Cody shook his head. "Can't. I have one of those gibberish password creators. And I don't remember the master password."

"So what are we going to do?" Patrick asked.

Cody shrugged.

"Hope my parents don't kill me," Cody said. "And that the link doesn't expire before then."

"It's going to be a *long* day," Patrick mumbled.

It *was* a long day.

Cody couldn't focus in any class. He kept trying to recall his password, but there was no way to remember. The master password was written on a note card. In his bedroom. Without it, he was locked out.

He wasn't just trying to focus on remembering his password so he could check his email—though that was definitely the *main* reason. He was trying to focus on that, and only that, so he could ignore the inevitable confrontation with his parents.

When the final bell rang, he made his way back to Mr. Kearns's room.

Mr. Kearns wasn't alone.

Cody's mom and dad were standing there as well.

"**I have never been more disappointed in you in my entire life**," his mom said—again—as they drove home.

They lived only a few blocks away, but his parents didn't let him walk. They also weren't driving straight home—they circled around town, forcing him to sit and listen as they berated him.

"I'm sorry," he said.

"And all this over a stupid *theme park*," his dad said for the hundredth time.

It isn't stupid, he wanted to say. "I'm sorry," he repeated instead.

"No phone. It's going away until you've earned it."

"But!"

"No!" his dad roared. "We're done. End of discussion. You're grounded for the rest of the weekend, too."

Cody bit his tongue. He knew grumbling and fighting wouldn't make it any better.

He slouched back in his seat and stared out the window as his parents continued to fight—first yelling at him, then at each other when they started throwing blame for being bad parents.

He was stuck.

Forever.

It didn't end when he got home.

The moment they pulled in the drive and he tried to hide in his room, his dad intercepted him.

"Oh, no, you don't," he said. His dad stormed ahead of him, pounding up the stairs.

Cody looked to his mom, but she wasn't any consolation. She just shrugged and walked into the kitchen. Worried, Cody followed his dad up to his bedroom.

His dad was on a rampage.

"You can't!" Cody yelled as his dad ripped down one of his mock-ups for a Tilt-A-Whirl reinvention.

"Watch me," his dad replied. He ripped down another drawing. "I'm sick of you wasting your time on this nonsense. From now on, you're going to be focused on school and nothing else, got it?"

Cody stared, openmouthed, as he watched his dad rip down more and more of his drawings.

Tears filled his eyes.

"Please," he whispered.

"Oh, now you're *crying*?"

Cody wiped his tears away. His dad didn't stop. He didn't stop until every piece of paper was torn off the walls—even papers that weren't theme park related—and crumpled on the floor. He eyed the roller coaster models and dioramas. Cody's heart lurched in fear.

But his dad must have thought it wasn't worth the cleanup or hassle. He turned and left without a word, slamming Cody's door shut behind him.

Only then did Cody let himself actually cry.

His dream was over.

This was reality. And no matter what Mr. Kearns had said, he didn't want to be a part of it.

Later that night, Cody realized he wasn't willing to accept this as his reality.

He kept staring over at the diorama on his desk, the one of an entire theme park he'd made for class. This *wasn't* a waste of time.

This was his life. And he wasn't going to let anyone get in the way of it.

Emboldened, he snuck downstairs. His parents had been asleep for hours, and he tiptoed down to the guest room. On the way, he grabbed the secret key from a jewelry box on the kitchen windowsill.

There was an old desk in the guest room, and when he opened the locked drawer with the key, he found his phone on top of a pile of tax returns and other boring paperwork. His phone was still on.

It glowed when he opened the drawer.

A dozen notifications. Most from Patrick, asking if he was still alive. And one more from ESCAPE.

FINAL CHANCE. YOU HAVE THREE HOURS.

It was time-stamped over two hours ago.

Cody's heart leaped into his chest as he finally, *finally*, opened the first email.

His heart didn't stop leaping, either, as he scanned the message.

And the next.

And the next.

The words weren't computing. They were like a foreign language. Like trying to read in a dream.

This couldn't be real.

This couldn't be happening.

All he caught were the words **Congratulations** and **Winner** and **Chance of a lifetime!**

And another phrase.

Confirm your spot before midnight, or miss out forever!

It was 11:59.

Hastily, he clicked the link for registration.

The internet dragged. The site took forever to load.

"Come on come on come on," he muttered, tapping his foot impatiently.

The clock turned.

Midnight.

The site loaded.

Cody Baxter!
Your reservation has been confirmed!
Prepare to escape all your worries.
Prepare to let your wildest dreams run free.
Your driver will be outside your residence at
8 a.m. sharp.
Your adventure is about to begin!

Cody slumped back. He took a breath for what felt like the first time in hours. Every single part of him shook, and he couldn't tell if it was shock or excitement.

He was doing it.

He was going.

Tomorrow, he was going to ESCAPE.

He didn't sleep at all for the rest of the night. He hid his phone back in the drawer and snuck back upstairs. He had already decided he wasn't going to tell his parents he'd won. They would never let him go, especially if they knew that he had broken the rules and stolen his phone back. They would never know, because he was leaving, and he honestly didn't plan on coming back. *How* he would manage that, he wasn't certain. He just knew that the moment he got to ESCAPE, all his problems would be solved. They had to be.

And his parents were one of his biggest problems.

For the first time in his life, Cody was grateful that his parents didn't care about him. He stuffed his backpack with clothes and even filled a duffel bag with the leftovers. He snuck out the side door at 7:50.

He wondered how he was going to manage this, if he'd have to wait in the bushes for his driver to show up.

But the moment he stepped outside, he saw the sleek black car out front. The driver stepped out. An equally sleek man in a black suit and black sunglasses looked him up and down.

"Cody Baxter?" the man asked.

Cody nodded and hurried over to the car. He looked over his shoulder. He hoped his parents didn't look out the window.

"Identification?" the man asked.

Cody fumbled in his pocket and pulled out his school ID. The man looked it over, then handed it back.

"Get in."

Cody narrowed his eyes. He might have been excited, and in a rush from fear of being discovered, but he knew better than to get in the car with a stranger.

"Do *you* have identification?" he asked.

The man's stoic demeanor split into a grin.

He reached into his pocket and pulled out his ID. But it wasn't a driver's license. It was an ID issued by ESCAPE.

"My driver number will match the number listed in your email," the driver—whose name was Kevin Merrill—said. He raised an eyebrow. "You *do* have that email, don't you?"

Cody looked at the man's ID again. He vaguely

remembered a driver number in his email, yes. But he wasn't about to go back inside and confirm.

"I, yes," Cody said.

"Did you want to double-check?" the man asked. "I mean, I do know you're Cody Baxter, you're twelve years old, you live in this house with your mom and dad and attend Judkins Middle School. You registered for the ESCAPE giveaway ten minutes after it opened, and you have interacted with every social media post we've added. Except for the last two, which—coincidentally—announced your invitation, as well as the closing of the contest, in that order."

Cody's mouth dropped open.

"You know all that?"

The man pulled out his phone and opened a document that showed Cody's photo and all of his details. Only a small portion of the things listed were things he'd entered on the registration form. The rest . . . *how in the world do they know so much about me?*

"We do our homework," Kevin said. "Are you ready? We're on a schedule."

Cody nodded.

Kevin took his bags and put them in the trunk. He opened the door for Cody, and Cody slipped in.

"Comfy?" Kevin asked when he got in the front seat.

"Totally," Cody replied. The back seat was luxurious leather, with soft ambient lighting that changed color.

"There's a cooler in the middle," Kevin said. "And a bunch of snacks in case you didn't get breakfast. We can stop if you need anything, but we're already pushing it time-wise. Okay then, let's go."

He pulled out of the driveway.

Cody didn't watch his house fade away. He didn't stare out the window at his classmates as they wandered to school.

He dug into the snacks and settled back in his seat. He felt . . . he didn't know how he felt. He'd never felt like this before.

Important? Catered to?

Is this what famous people feel like? he wondered. *I could get used to this. And maybe, after ESCAPE, I will.*

He closed his eyes.

When he fell asleep, he dreamed of golden roller coasters high up in the clouds.

Either Cody slept for a lot longer than he meant to, or the driver drove a lot faster than he should have, because when Cody opened his eyes again, they were pulling up in front of a dilapidated concrete wall in what looked like some abandoned industrial district.

And Cody really, really had to pee.

"Where are we?" Cody asked.

"Our destination," Kevin said.

He got out of the driver's seat and walked around the car, opening Cody's door before grabbing his stuff from the trunk.

"Are you sure?" Cody asked. He got out slowly. "This doesn't look like a theme park."

In fact, the place looked like the exact *opposite* of a theme park. Abandoned warehouses and factories towered around them, all rusted out and broken and abandoned. Chunks of glass littered the street, and newspapers crumpled around bent lampposts.

"I'm just the driver, kid," Kevin said. "Enjoy."

Before Cody could stop him, Kevin got in the car and drove off.

"Wait!" Cody yelled out. But the car didn't stop. In seconds, the sleek black car disappeared around a corner, and Cody was alone. No one walked the streets. No one worked in the factories. This couldn't be it. This couldn't be right.

Had he made a mistake?

Was this all a trap?

Even if there *was* a giant theme park hidden behind this wall, he couldn't hear it. No music or laughter or clicks of a roller coaster. Just the quiet and the cold and the dirt.

For a moment, he thought maybe it was a test. Maybe he needed to wait here until a magical door opened up. Then another cold breeze blew over him, wrapping newspapers around his ankles, and the thought seemed even more unlikely.

Okay. Maybe he'd walk. Just a little bit. Maybe there was a gate or something. Maybe the driver had screwed up. He reached into his pocket before realizing he didn't have his phone. He couldn't call or text or see where he was. His heart dropped. He was in real trouble. He considered just starting to yell out at the top of his lungs. Maybe someone would come rescue him.

At the very least, maybe he'd find a bathroom.

Then he saw the car.

It was nondescript. Black and sleek, just like his own had been, with tinted windows and generic license plates.

He looked around. Considered running. But there was nowhere to go. If this was a trap, if this was where he was captured . . .

The car slowed down. Stopped a few feet ahead of him. *I should run. I should at least try to run.*

The door opened, and Cody winced, expecting the worst.

"Hey!" someone called out. It took a second to realize it was a kid. "Are you here for ESCAPE?"

Cody knew that voice before the guy even got out of the
car. Jayson had been all over the radio lately, his hit single "Because You Love to Love Me" number one for
the last three weeks. Jayson had been one of the first
people invited to ESCAPE, and had even done a radio
interview talking about how excited he was to go. Cody
was embarrassed to admit that he'd probably listened to
it just as many times as he'd heard Jayson sing.

When Jayson stepped out of the car, Cody felt like
he was somehow in an alternate reality.

"Yeah," Cody replied after realizing Jayson had
asked if he was also here for the park. "But I don't
know if it's the right place."

He gestured to the high wall and the dirty factories. Jayson didn't seem dissuaded. He stepped out of the car with two big roller bags and the driver was off a second later, just like Cody's own mysterious ride.

"I'm Jayson," he said, holding out his hand.

It was such a simple gesture, but Cody was stunned. It took a moment for his body to kick into motion. He reached out and took Jayson's hand, wondering at how surreal this all felt.

Jayson was exactly like Cody had seen online. He was half-Japanese, half-white, with choppy black hair streaked with magenta, and an easy smile. He wore all black—everything drapey and gauzy but somehow fitting him perfectly. Probably handmade. Heck, even his suitcases looked designer.

"I'm Cody," Cody said awkwardly. "Cody Baxter. I love your songs."

He hated himself the moment he said it. He felt himself blush, but oddly, so did Jayson.

"Thanks," Jayson replied. "But here I'm just a kid. Like you. K?"

Cody nodded. Though he didn't think Jayson would ever be just like him.

He looked down at his own thin Henley shirt, his faded jeans. He had thought he looked good enough for a strong first impression this morning, but now he wasn't so sure. In that moment, he knew that even his best clothes wouldn't compare to the worst that all the stars were bringing. He hadn't thought of it before, but he realized then that even though he and the other normal kids would be sharing a park with celebrities, supposedly in the spirit of kinship, something as simple as clothing would keep them separated as strongly as this concrete wall.

Speaking of. Cody glanced around. "Do you know where the entrance is?"

"Nah," Jayson said casually. "But it's gotta be around here somewhere."

He said it so calmly. Then again, he was probably used to everything going his way. He was a celebrity, after all. Life didn't hit him the same way it did Cody.

For a brief moment, Cody wanted to hate him. Then Jayson smiled, and the anger dissolved.

"Glad you're here, though," Jayson said. "This place creeps me the heck out. Kinda feels like we're the last kids alive, doesn't it? Should we try to find the entrance?"

Cody nodded, unable to speak. Jayson—the number-one pop star Jayson—was happy that Cody was there. If this kept up, he'd be floating over the wall.

The two of them slowly began walking along the wall, both of them staring up at it in wonder.

"You just got your ticket, right?" Jayson asked.

Cody hadn't even considered that the famous kids would have been paying attention to who else had gotten in.

"Yeah," Cody said. Ugh, couldn't he say something

smarter in response? "Last night. I didn't even get a chance to tell my friends."

"They're going to be so jealous," Jayson replied. "I swear, like, half my friend group stopped talking to me when they found out." He must have noticed the fear that crossed Cody's face—*I never told them, and I don't have a chance to tell them. They're going to hate me!* "I'm sure that won't be the case for you, though. My friends are pretty flaky."

"Sorry," Cody replied.

Cody was spared further awkward conversation by another car. This one was white and sporty. It pulled up beside the two of them, and the back window rolled down a crack.

"ESCAPE?"

The voice was quiet and feminine, lilting with an accent that definitely wasn't from around here.

"Yeah," Jayson said. "You're in the right place." He looked around. "I think."

Then the voice clicked, and the door opened to reveal the girl of Cody's dreams: Inga.

Inga was a famous Norwegian singer and actress. Her hits had topped every chart for years, and she'd even starred in a few blockbuster movies. She was gorgeous. Long blonde hair pulled back in a ponytail and bright blue eyes like ice crystals. When she stepped out of the car, Cody's heart fluttered like never before.

And that's when it hit him. He was here. With two celebrities. One of whom he'd had a crush on for months. Which meant ESCAPE was really happening. He was really doing it. He, Cody Baxter, was about to have the time of his life.

Then he realized that both Jayson and Inga were staring at him expectantly, and he realized someone had asked him a question.

"Huh?" he asked.

"His name is Cody," Jayson said.

"Oh," Inga said. She didn't shake his hand. "Nice to meet you. I'm Inga."

"I know," Cody replied.

And just like that, the little happy bubble popped. Because Inga knew he wasn't special, and he definitely hadn't made a good first impression on her.

He felt his cheeks flush with embarrassment. So much for that one. Maybe he should just turn around and walk home before he could make more of a fool of himself.

He was about to do just that.

And then there was a rumble, and a hidden panel in the wall slowly slid to the side, revealing a silvery, light-filled hallway and a man in a pristine white suit.

"Welcome," he said, his voice booming with excitement and his arms spreading wide, "to ESCAPE."

Cody couldn't wipe the grin from his face.

Even though he'd just embarrassed himself in front of what were probably two of the coolest kids he'd ever met, the moment that door slid open, all the excitement from before bubbled back to the surface. The man who stepped out of the silvery room was maybe the same age as Cody's dad, with tousled black hair and warm brown eyes. He looked like he hadn't slept or shaved in a bit, but that didn't make him seem any less excited to see them. He held his arms out to the sides as if giving them all a hug.

"My name is Mr. Gould," he said. "I am the park's creator, and you must be . . ." He tapped his lips thoughtfully, and once more Cody felt that tiny sliver of fear—that even though he was here, his lack of fame would single him out as a nobody. "Cody Baxter," Mr. Gould said, pointing at him. Cody's heart swelled. "Jayson Torn. And, last but not least, dear Inga Andersdottir. What a pleasure." He looked to their bags. "Here, come in, come in. I'll have my attendants help you."

He gestured, and three people came out from the room, wearing slick navy uniforms with silver embroidery, ESCAPE emblazoned on the chest. They looked a lot fancier than any theme park attendant Cody had seen before.

Then again, he had always known that this would be unlike any park he'd ever attended. That was the whole point.

The uniformed helpers grabbed their bags effortlessly. The guy who took Cody's smiled at him warmly.

"Welcome," he said softly.

"Thanks," Cody replied. Then he wondered if he should tip the guy for his help. At least, that's what he'd seen his parents do when they all went on a fancy vacation a few years back, before the fighting began.

"We are still waiting for a few more attendees," Mr. Gould said, turning and leading them into the room, "but we are very excited to have you with us. The park will officially open just after our reception meal this afternoon. After that, you will have seven full days to explore!"

Cody and the others stepped into the silvery room. Even with all seven of them in there, it was spacious enough to fit another dozen. The walls were all sleek silver, and light came from a bunch of starlike dots along the ceiling. The moment they were all inside, the door slid shut behind them, and Cody found himself staring at his own reflection.

He was still grinning.

So were Jayson and Inga.

He saw Mr. Gould press his hand to the wall, and a few blue lights buzzed to life. Then, with a rumble, the room began to move. Not up, toward the top of the wall. But *down*.

"I'm sure you all have many questions," Mr. Gould said. "And I promise you they will all be answered in time. For now, though, we have a brief intake procedure, after which you will begin your experience."

The elevator stopped so smoothly that Cody didn't realize it had stopped moving until the door before him opened, revealing a rather ordinary-looking reception area, complete with gray carpeting, houndstooth-print chairs, and fake potted plants. A few of the chairs already had kids sitting on them.

Cody was honestly a little disappointed. It looked—and smelled—like a doctor's office.

Mr. Gould ushered the new arrivals into the waiting area.

"But what about our things?" Inga asked. Cody turned to see the three assistants disappearing behind the elevator doors with all their bags.

"They will be delivered to your rooms," Mr. Gould said. "This way."

He stepped into the waiting area. A few of the kids looked up. Some were nervous. Others excited. There were maybe a dozen in all, but the space was so large that it looked empty.

Cody had to wonder just how many kids the park was meant to hold at full capacity. It was clear, from the size of this place, that they were expecting thousands. And to think, it would only be one hundred for the first week. No waiting, no lines.

Well, no waiting except for right now.

Mr. Gould led them to a long desk, where a few receptionists were waiting with ready smiles. Cody and the others were given clipboards with some very official-looking paperwork attached. Mr. Gould told them to fill out the forms, and a nurse would be in to assist them afterward. Then there would be lunch, and they would be told what to do from there.

Cody didn't want to wait that long. He could barely contain the excited adrenaline coursing through his body. There was no hint of the park just beyond these walls, no clue as to what they might expect. He was *this close*, and everything was even more mysterious than before. But he sat down with his paperwork and tried to focus on the questions. He was so hyped he barely noticed Inga and Jayson sitting beside him.

"They sure do ask a lot for a theme park, don't they?" Jayson muttered.

Cody had noticed a few different celebrities in the waiting area, including some YouTube stars that he figured Jayson and Inga would know. Why were they hanging out with him, now that they didn't have to?

"Yeah," Cody said. Then he remembered he'd only been using one-word answers, and decided to take the plunge. "I feel like we're trying out for the Olympics or something."

Jayson nodded. "Right? This is nuts."

Inga laughed. "Don't they know not to ask a lady how much she weighs?"

"Don't worry," Jayson said. "I won't tell a soul."

Cody skimmed over the questions. "I think that measurements are the least intrusive, honestly."

Because in addition to the normal questions like body weight and height and age, there were other, stranger questions. Like your diet and caffeine intake and sleep patterns and favorite movie genres. And . . .

"'What are you most afraid of?'" Inga voiced. She looked from the paper to Cody. Her blue eyes . . .

Cody hated to admit just how entrancing they were. "I don't know if I want to answer that question. Why are they asking us that?"

"Because they try to tailor the park to whatever experiences you need," Cody answered. "If you're scared of clowns, for instance, and you want to go into the haunted house, they'll make sure clowns show up."

"That sounds dangerous," Jayson replied.

Cody shrugged. For the first time in forever, he no longer felt like a fanboy for knowing everything there was to know about ESCAPE.

How weird was it that he was in a position to explain things to *celebrities*?

"It doesn't have to be dangerous," he said, pointing to a series of check boxes. "See? Right here. If you don't want to be scared, you can tick the box there and they'll make sure *not* to have the thing you're afraid of appear. They track every single person in the park at all times, so there's no risk of anything bad happening." Cody grinned. "Unless you want something bad to happen, that is."

Inga looked shocked.

"Why would anyone want something bad to happen?" she asked.

"Because," Cody said, amazed at his own confidence, "if nothing bad happens, you have no reason to escape."

9

The written questions were only the beginning.

Jayson was talking about his flight from New York when a nurse came over and called him to the back room. Jayson waved nervously as he walked away.

"He's cute, no?" Inga asked.

Cody started.

"Um . . ."

She seemed to notice his expression. "Don't worry. You are just as cute."

Cody felt his cheeks catch fire.

"Um, thanks," he muttered, his few words tripping over his tongue. At least he had the mental clarity not to say, *You're really pretty, too.*

"You know a lot about this place," Inga said. "It is impressive. Why did you want to come here?"

Cody *almost* said everything he knew he shouldn't. That his parents were always fighting and he was a nobody at school and he needed a chance to get away from all that. That he wanted to build a theme park more than anything else in the world. That he wanted to make cool friends who would take him and Laura and Patrick away from their boring lives. That even though he was glad to be here, he felt bad that his friends couldn't join him.

He didn't say any of that.

Instead, he lied. Sort of.

"I thought it sounded fun," he said with a shrug that probably looked forced and not nonchalant. "You know. Something different. I was bored of the parks at home and I figured, why not? I mean, it's cool I'm part of this group, but I would have come no matter what. Adventure's sort of my thing. And yeah, I researched a lot. But only because I wanted to make sure it wasn't bogus. Don't want to waste my time."

He didn't know why, but she almost looked disappointed by his answer.

"What about you?" he asked.

If her eyes sparkled before, now the shine seemed to go out.

"I needed to get away."

Then, before he could ask her what she meant by that, a nurse came over and called him to the back room.

He looked back as he walked away.

Inga wasn't watching him go.

He'd really messed up.

It definitely felt like going to the doctor.

Cody sat in a tiny, somewhat cold room while a nurse in crisp blue scrubs asked him a bunch of questions about allergies and stress levels and diet and exercise habits, all the while taking his blood pressure and checking his reflexes and shining lights into his eyes.

At least he didn't have to pee in a cup.

He wanted to ask what this had to do with ESCAPE, and why he needed a full physical exam to go to an adventure park, but he was so caught up in the excitement that he just went along for the ride. So he sat there and answered the questions and tried not to think about Inga, and what he might have said wrong, and how he could fix it later. *If* he could fix it later.

Clearly, he wasn't so good at not thinking about her.

Then the nurse repeated a question, and he was snapped back to reality.

"Are you okay with needles?" she said for the third time.

"Oh, yeah." It was a lie. He hated needles. But again, he wasn't about to let anything get in the way of him and ESCAPE.

The nurse nodded, as though that was enough, and handed him yet another clipboard with a form attached.

"For the initial launch of the park," she explained, "every attendee is given a biotracker in the form of an injection. It's completely safe, and will break down and pass through your system in about two weeks naturally. It will let us monitor things like heart rate, adrenaline levels, that sort of thing. And ensures that we can always find you in case of emergency." She pointed to the form. "That release waiver says that I've told you, and that you sign off on the procedure."

"Procedure?" he asked, imagining a hacksaw.

"Just a shot." She held up a tiny needle filled with fluorescent-blue liquid. "Over in a second."

He bit his lip. Signed the paper.

"Very good," she said, taking the form. "Now, this won't hurt a bit."

She stuck in the needle.

It didn't hurt a bit. It hurt much more than a bit.

10

"Welcome, everyone!"

Mr. Gould's voice echoed through the cafeteria, his image projected on a screen behind his podium.

Cody sat at a table beside Jayson and—miraculously—Inga, as well as a few other faces he recognized but hadn't said hello to yet. He tried to keep from rubbing his arm. He couldn't tell if the shot hurt because it had been painful or if it was simply because he hated getting shots.

He was pleased to see that Jayson kept poking at his own blue bandage. At least Cody wasn't the only one.

"I hope you are as excited as I am for the experience that is about to unfold," Mr. Gould continued. "In a few hours, you will embark on a journey like no other. If you can dream it, ESCAPE will help you achieve it." He waved his hand, and the screen behind him changed.

The new image was computer-rendered, and it showed kids running through the park, laughing and jumping. There were roller coasters and hot-air balloons, wandering dinosaurs and floating pirate ships. Even though Cody had seen similar renderings before, being this close to actually *living* it made his breath catch and his heart race.

"As you know, we have only two rules in this park. One: Have fun. And two: No adults allowed. As such, all interactions will be through service monitors placed in convenient locations throughout the park." The rendition showed two kids approaching what looked like an ATM. "Through these, you can communicate with us back at the command center or access the full database of what ESCAPE has to offer, from maps to games directories to where you can find late-night pizza." On-screen, the kids were swiping through various options, including delicious-looking meals—sushi and pizza and burgers, all of them reminding him that all he'd had to eat so far was a granola bar.

"We will, of course, be monitoring your activity from here, so we *do* recommend you be on your best behavior. Just know it is merely a precaution, and we will always be on hand if there is any sort of emergency. Not that we foresee that happening. ESCAPE is perfectly safe, even if it feels dangerous at times. We have everything under control."

The screen changed, now showing many of the attractions Cody had seen before, and a few he had not. Kids paragliding over erupting volcanoes while pterodactyls flew past. Fighting one another with laser swords on a spaceship darting through the cosmos. Deep-sea diving while a shark loomed in the background. Transforming into huge robots and dueling in a junkyard. Each of the scenarios got Cody's pulse racing. Soon, very soon, he'd be doing all that and more.

He glanced over to Inga and Jayson, and wondered if he'd be lucky enough to explore it all with them. They were both just as entranced by the screen as he was, their eyes big and huge smiles on their faces.

"Now," Dr. Gould said, "you must all be starving, so let me briefly go over the basics of your time at ESCAPE. As you have learned, you will all be staying in private suites while on-site. They are located here, next to the main entrance." The screen changed to show a huge map with two blinking red dots. "Many of you asked what sort of clothing you should bring, and our response was always silence. That is because, as part of your experience, you have all been given a special uniform."

The screen changed again, this time showing two rotating models, each in what looked like a superhero suit—black and covered with futuristic lines like circuits. His heart dropped. He couldn't imagine feeling comfortable walking around in *that*.

"These suits are specially designed to seamlessly blend with the park's experience. With them, you will be able to fly, transform, and wield powers beyond your wildest dreams. The suits will track your activities and scores, and—as a special extra incentive—the kid with the highest score at the end of the week will win a very special prize. The suits are also climate-controlled to keep you at the perfect body temperature. In addition, you will be granted special smartwatches." The models now zoomed in to their wrists, showcasing a thick round watch face with a bunch of swirling images. "These, in addition to the monitors scattered throughout the park, will help guide you through your adventure. I trust you will find the interface quite intuitive.

"Once you are equipped, you will be free to do as you please throughout the park. There are no curfews. No rules. No money exchanged. Everything within the park is included in your admission. Eat as much as you like, whenever you like. Play until sunrise and keep going. This is your week to do whatever you please and live life to the fullest. At the end, there will be a brief survey, and we hope you will give us honest feedback so we can continue to make the park better for future children to enjoy.

"So please. Enjoy yourselves. Live fully. Let the outside world melt away. Here, you can truly escape!"

Fireworks exploded on the screen behind him, and confetti burst down from the ceiling in glittering metallic clouds. Everyone applauded. Cody loudest of all.

Panels along the walls slid open, revealing various food vendors of all types. Burritos and sandwiches, burgers and salads, kimchi and pho and dishes Cody had never even heard of before. And best of all, they were all free.

"Shall we?" Jayson asked him, nodding to the growing lines of kids.

"Let's," Inga said. She hadn't really said anything to Cody, but so long as she was speaking to Jayson, and Jayson was hanging with Cody, it was close enough.

They got up together and grabbed lunch, chatting with other kids along the way. Cody met a pro skateboarder name Leah and a math genius who'd been awarded some medal, along with the kid of a really famous celebrity whose latest movie Cody had seen a dozen times.

Because he was with Jayson and Inga, Cody hadn't

met anyone who had been gifted a ticket by lottery. But they were easy to spot. They were the ones keeping to the edges, not really talking. Like him, they didn't feel like they fit in, even now. Mortals amid gods.

Unlike him, they hadn't been granted the lucky cards of meeting two stars before the park even opened. Right then, Cody felt incredibly grateful. Just having Jayson and Inga at his side made him confident enough to talk to others. Even though—truth be told—those kids often started speaking to Jayson or Inga, and then noticed Cody and said hello.

At least it was something.

Cody heaped his plate with scrambled eggs, fried rice, a cheeseburger, and a few donuts. Inga eyed it suspiciously, but didn't say anything. Jayson got nearly as much food as he did. After a small chuckle, so did Inga.

Their trio attracted a few followers, and when they sat down for lunch, they found their side of the table pretty much packed.

Cody felt strange being the center of so much attention, even if only on the periphery. It made him feel popular. The trouble was, it was too crowded for him to actually talk to his newfound friends, and it made him worry that they would find someone more interesting and leave him.

Jayson talked about life in New York, and how

he hated how crowded and expensive it was but there was so much to do it was easy to ignore it. *It's just the cost of living an adventure,* he said. Which was definitely not something Cody would have ever thought about his own life.

"What do you think the prize is?" one of the new guys asked.

"Money, probably," Jayson said. "Or, like, I don't know. An interview with the *New York Times* or something."

"We don't need money," someone else pitched in. A girl. "At least, not all of us."

Cody didn't look up from his plate, but he could feel the speaker's eyes bore into him. Jayson, at least, didn't seem fazed by the remark.

"C'mon," Jayson said. "There's no such thing as too much money. Especially when you have a staff of ten and a family of six depending on you to earn enough for all of them."

Jayson seemed to naturally want to drift to the center of everyone's attention. He started telling stories about all the big music events he'd gone to, the red-carpet premieres, the late-night recording sessions with other famous musicians. He kept glancing at Inga, waiting for her to chip in with her own stories, but she stayed silent.

Cody noticed.

"And you?" one of the new kids asked. Cody knew her by face alone. This was Meg-A, a singer who'd risen to fame seemingly overnight with a single pop hit and a music video of animated rabbits.

It took Cody a moment to realize she was talking to him.

"What?" Everyone's eyes were on him, and he realized he was already blushing wildly.

"What do you do?" Meg-A's fingernails were shaped like knives, and her voice had a tone to match. She had aqua streaks in her light brown hair and fierce blue eyeshadow, like she was ready to take the stage. "Or are you one of the lucky losers who snuck in?"

Cody felt his blush deepen, words lodging in his throat. Half a dozen celebrities stared at him, waiting for him to give an answer that everyone knew would spell out just how normal and boring he was.

Then Jayson hooked an arm over Cody's shoulders.

"You haven't heard of my man Cody?" Jayson asked incredulously.

"No," Meg-A snapped. "Should I have?"

Jayson just laughed.

"The important ones have," he said. He smiled broadly. "So maybe it's no surprise that you haven't."

He pushed himself up to standing and grabbed his tray.

"Come on, Cody. Let's go find where we get our uniforms. For some reason, I've lost my appetite."

He glared pointedly at Meg-A. Cody stayed silent, but he didn't object. He grabbed his own tray and stood.

Cody didn't know what shocked him more: the fact that Jayson had stood up for him, or the fact that Inga quietly followed them from the cafeteria.

"You didn't have to do that," Cody said.

They were outside the cafeteria, following a bunch of signs that said UNIFORMS: THIS WAY.

"What?" Jayson asked. "Put Meg-A in her place? Please. We've had a Twitter war going for months." He winked. "It wasn't just for you, don't worry. Though you *are* my friend, which means I'm gonna stand up for you." He looked to Inga. "Both of you."

"But you just met us," Cody said.

Jayson shrugged.

"I have good intuition," he said. "And I know you're both good people. Like you, Cody. You aren't here for the fame. You're here out of love. And Inga, I've read your story. You're not here for the same reasons everyone else is, either."

"Why *are* you here?" Cody asked, recalling their earlier conversation.

Inga didn't seem to want to answer. She watched her feet and bit her lip, looking so much more unassuming than she did in her music videos. In every clip he'd seen of her, even in interviews, she was powerful and assured and mysterious.

Cody immediately regretted asking. If *that* didn't upset her enough to avoid him, he couldn't imagine what would.

"I want something more," she finally said, glancing at Cody. "To be in a place where people like me for who I am, and not for what the internet made me. It is tiring pretending all the time."

"I know what you mean," Cody said. "I mean, not for the same reasons, obviously. But yeah. Sometimes I feel like all I do is pretend."

"I know," Inga said. The seriousness in her voice made him think that she truly did know. Though he couldn't figure out how or why.

"Come on, guys," Jayson said. He jogged backward a few steps ahead of them, the grin still plastered on his face. "We're in the coolest place on earth! You know the motto: 'Here, you can truly escape!'"

"I hope so," Inga said.

"I *know* so. Everything that's behind us is in the past. We've got the chance to have the time of our lives. And I, for one, plan on living it up. You with me?"

"Totally," Cody said. Despite the seriousness of the previous conversation, a grin lit up his face. Partly for Jayson's enthusiasm, and partly because . . .

"Is that the park?" Inga asked, awestruck.

They had just passed in front of a huge window overlooking the park. "Wow" was all Jayson could say. Cody just nodded silently.

Cody had dreamed of this place for months, but ESCAPE was still bigger and grander than the wildest of those dreams.

He could see the entire park from here, and what he saw made his breath catch. Coasters as tall as skyscrapers stretched up into the clouds, their rails glittering like metallic rainbows in the sunlight, and around those rails, enormous birds were flapping and circling.

No, not birds—*pterodactyls!* They swooped and dove toward the amusements below:

A tilted, teetering haunted house that flickered with green inner light.

A massive pyramid covered in enormous hieroglyphs.

A glittering lake dotted with pirate ships, and something serpentine and monstrous curling beneath the waves.

A forest of gnarled trees and lurking shadows, complete with a castle poking from the canopy.

A gleaming silver spaceship, steam billowing from its engines as it awaited its passengers for some intergalactic voyage.

Everywhere he looked was something new and impossible, inviting and exhilarating.

It was waiting for them.

For him.

"I think this will be better than I could have ever imagined," Inga said breathlessly. She looked at Cody. And smiled.

After what felt like *ages*, Cody and his friends were finally gathered in front of the huge iron gates leading into the park. They'd taken yet another elevator down to get to the main level, and the doors had opened into a sort of holding area—in front of them, the iron gates kept the park just out of reach. Behind them, an impossibly high concrete wall stretched up into the heavens. The gate curved around them, sealing them into the enclosure. For the first time, he felt a little claustrophobic—everything else so far had been spread out and inviting, but this part, standing shoulder to shoulder with the other kids, made him feel like a cow in a factory.

But his misgivings were small, and it was hard to be

worried with everything that awaited in front of him.

Beyond the gate, a wide boulevard led to the heart of the park. Trees lined the cobblestone road, along with statues and fountains of dragons and griffins, knights on horseback and moving robots. Banners stretched overhead, welcoming them in for the grand opening. He could just see the tops of the rides over the trees, could just smell the delicious food from the street vendors.

The air in here felt different.

Electric.

Alive.

He looked around to the others. Everyone was in uniform, and everyone was filled with the same giddy energy as he was. A few kids were bobbing up and down on their toes. One or two even had tears of excitement in their eyes. He spotted Meg-A in the crowd—she was taller than everyone, and that eye-shadow was hard to miss—and he was surprised to see that even she was smiling like a little kid.

"What's taking them so long?" Jayson asked. "My body is ready!"

"I do not know," Inga whispered.

They'd only been down here a few minutes, but the excitement was quickly being replaced by confusion. Why were they still stuck in here? Caged. Kenneled. Cody was starting to worry something was wrong. It was clear Inga thought the same. She looked up to the wall behind them.

That wall stretched all the way around the park, closing them off from the outside world—Cody had seen that from the window up above. He guessed that he was currently a hundred feet or so below street level, though it was hard to be certain. He couldn't see any of the outside buildings, and the sky seemed way too close for that. What he saw warred with what he thought to be true.

All he knew was, the only way out of the park was through the huge steel elevator doors that were sealed shut behind them.

It would just take one slight electrical malfunction, one blackout, and they'd all be stuck here forever . . .

Before he could worry about that, though, the air above the gate flickered, and a second later a hologram of Mr. Gould's smiling face pushed all of Cody's worries away.

"Is everyone ready?" he asked.

"Yeah!" the crowd cried out.

Mr. Gould grinned. "Hmmm," he said. "You don't sound too enthusiastic. Perhaps we should get another group in . . ."

At that, everyone started whooping and hollering, cheering so loud that a flock of parrots rose from a nearby tree and flew away.

Mr. Gould laughed. "That's more like it," he said. "Okay then. On your marks—"

Cody's skin was electric. This was it. This. Was. *It!* He just wished Patrick and Laura were here to experience this with him.

"Come onnnnnn," Jayson groaned beside him. Cody laughed. Even if his friends back home weren't here, he was grateful he had new friends to enjoy this with.

"Get set—"

Briefly, the warnings of Mr. Kearns and Laura flitted through his thoughts. *What if this place isn't as cool as I want it to be? What if it doesn't change anything? What if I don't actually—* "ESCAPE!"

On cue, more confetti burst from the statues around them, and the great gates swung open. Fireworks exploded in the sky, and music blasted from hidden speakers. Jayson took him by the arm. Inga took his hand.

Surrounded by the most famous, coolest kids around, he ran into the adventure of his dreams.

Cody was perfectly overwhelmed.

The crowd of kids rushed the gates like a Black Friday sale, pressing him forward and into the park amid shouts and excited laughter. He let himself get caught up in the emotion, laughing and yelling with all the rest as they raced down the street.

Each statue they passed saluted them in its own unique way: The dragons breathed billows of green flame, the knights waved their lances, the robots spun their heads and flashed their eyes. Fountains sprayed intricate displays and music spurred them on, forward, down the boulevard and into the first plaza.

It was here that Cody paused in wonder, Inga and Jayson halting at his sides.

The place was enormous and round, the ground

inlaid with glittering tiles like a great compass rose. But rather than pointing north or east, there were a dozen arms branching out, each pointing to an archway proclaiming which world lay beyond.

There was Ancient Egypt, the arch supported on sandstone pillars covered in hieroglyphs and carvings of pharaohs and ancient gods, a pyramid rising in the distance.

Intergalactic Adventure's sign was metallic and covered in blinking lights, with tiny rockets spiraling along the archway.

Over there was King Arthur's Kingdom, the stone sign supported by twin dragons that puffed smoke and glowered warningly at the kids running through.

There was also the Deep Sea Domain, where giant squids held a reef that spelled out its name.

And Prehistoric Paradise, where velociraptors held a wooden sign and Cody *swore* he saw a T. rex amble by in the distance.

And then there was the Haunted Hillside. *That* sign was made of bones, and a cold breeze billowed out. The trees obscuring the rides beyond were blackened and gnarled, flickering with ghostly green lights.

Cody's mind practically exploded with excitement.

"Where do you want to go first?" he asked.

"I don't even know," Jayson said breathlessly. "All of them? At once?"

Cody chuckled. But every second they waited was another second lost. There was so much to see, so much to *do*! Everyone else had already chosen which theme to go toward. It was now just him and Inga and Jayson standing in the entrance plaza.

Cody briefly looked up into the clear blue sky. And that's when he noticed something strange.

There were lines in the sky. Like a grid. Like the clouds and blue were all being projected onto a concrete wall. *Weird*. Were they still underground?

It didn't really matter. All that mattered was the experience in front of him.

"How about Ancient Egypt?" Inga suggested. "I've always wanted to see the pyramids. And I think less kids went that way."

"Great idea!" Cody exclaimed. And, still holding hands, the three of them ran past the dinosaur archway and into a land far, far from the one Cody had left behind.

The air here was hot and dry, and sand piled at the edges of the paths. Great pillars and statues of Egyptian deities and pharaohs lined the walkway. The great pyramid got closer with every step, but that wasn't what snared Cody's attention. The twisting pathway wasn't just dotted with statues. Ride entrances faced them every few feet. Only the stone archways were visible—the rides themselves sat hidden behind sandblasted walls, so no one could see what was in store. All they had to go on were the names arching above them: Pyramid Plummet, Terror of the Sphynx, Anubis Escape.

"Which should we try first?" Jayson asked.

"Something that doesn't involve going upside down," Cody admitted. "I'm still really full and don't want to spend my first day puking."

"Gross," Inga said, smiling along with Jayson. "And also, agreed."

After the lunchroom encounter, Cody decided he wasn't going to pretend to be something he wasn't, at least not around Inga and Jayson. They were his friends. And just like with his friends back home, he would be his normal, strange self.

Jayson considered his watch, then looked around. Now that everyone had spread out, the park seemed somewhat empty. Faint instrumental music played in the background, and Cody could occasionally hear someone calling out with glee. But otherwise, it was just them along the wide path, and a park of opportunities spread out around them. "Well," Jayson mused, "we could go about it two ways. We could find a directory and pick what we want to do. Or we could just start somewhere and work our way through."

"The second one," Cody said.

"Yeah," Inga agreed. "We have a full week. I'm sure we can hit up every ride in the park by then."

"I don't know about that," Cody warned. "From what I've heard, there are over three *hundred* rides here. We'd have to do more than forty rides a day to hit them all."

"Better start sooner than later," Jayson said with a grin. He pointed. "How about that one?"

Cody didn't even look to where Jayson was pointing before agreeing.

He knew that he would go anywhere with these two.

14

It turned out that Jayson had randomly picked a somewhat menacing first ride.

PYRAMID PLUMMET

It didn't sound like it would go upside down, but Cody feared that if this was one of those rides that dropped you a hundred feet, he'd still be losing his lunch.

"What do you think it will be?" Jayson asked as they meandered down the path. "A coaster or water ride or . . . ?"

Cody shrugged. He couldn't imagine what it would be, and he almost didn't want to. He wanted it to be a surprise.

The path to the ride twisted and turned through

high stone walls that nearly blocked out the blistering sun. Small lizards darted across the weathered stones, and scarabs scuttled around his feet. Cody wondered if they were real animals or animatronic. He also wondered if the heat was real, or part of his suit—it felt like it was a million degrees, even in the shade. He hadn't even considered that having a temperature-controlled suit could be used to make him *un*comfortable.

Eventually, the maze made one final turn and opened up. For the hundredth time that afternoon, his breath caught in his chest.

A massive pyramid loomed up in front of them, so tall it blotted out the sun. Rolling sand dunes stretched out on all sides, trailing off into a heatwave haze.

"*Impossible,*" Inga whispered. "Where is the rest of the park?"

Cody looked behind them.

"No way," he replied.

Because there was nothing there.

Just endless, blistering sands. No hallway leading back to the Egypt plaza. No hint of other rides. No scent of cooking foods.

No sounds but the wind brushing the sand.

No signs of life except for the three of them.

"I guess there's no chickening out now, huh?" Jayson said.

"Guess not," Cody replied. He looked back

toward the pyramid. Now that they were in the shadow of the colossal thing, he was actually kind of cold. "Which . . . any clue where the entrance is?"

On cue, a shadow shifted on the horizon beside them. At least, Cody thought there was something moving out there—it was hard to tell in the haze of heat. Inga noticed it, too.

"What's that?" she asked.

They squinted, watching the shape speed nearer and nearer.

It was fast.

Too fast.

"Um, should we run?" Jayson asked. "It's heading straight toward us."

"I don't know," Cody said. He took a hesitant step back. The object was *definitely* coming up fast, but he still couldn't tell what it was. "Maybe?"

A gust of wind blew a screen of sand in front of them, obscuring the incoming shadow. And when it cleared, they realized it wasn't a monster or something sinister. It was a buggy.

The car careened toward them, driverless, and skidded to a stop only a dozen feet away, kicking up a plume of sand in the process.

"Uck," Jayson groaned, spitting sand out of his mouth and trying to wipe it off his clothes. Which, Cody noticed, had suddenly become explorer's outfits—khaki pants and button-down shirts and brown boots. Very Indiana Jones.

"Whoa, look at you," Cody said.

Both Inga and Jayson quickly admired their new clothes—and Cody once more wondered how *any* of this was possible.

The buggy revved its engine.

"I think it wants us to get in," Cody said.

"I'm driving!" Jayson proclaimed. He jumped into the front seat.

"You wanna ride shotgun?" Cody asked Inga.

"I think I will stay in the back," she answered with a small smile. "In case there are spiderwebs where we are going."

Of course. The buggy would probably take them on a tour through the pyramid, and pyramids *always* equaled spiderwebs in the movies.

"I hate spiders," Cody replied. "And scorpions."

"Well then," Inga said, hopping into the back seat. "This should be a fun ride for you."

Cody laughed and jumped in beside Jayson.

"Okay then," Jayson said, "how do I—"

Before he could finish his sentence, the buggy revved its engine again. Seat belts snapped across their waists. The gear shifted automatically.

With a spray of sand, the buggy rocketed off, heading toward the heart of the pyramid.

Cody had thought the pyramid looked huge before, but as they neared, he realized just how awesome it truly was.

The sun was completely eclipsed by its shadow, and it stretched so far up that by the time they reached the base, he had to crane his neck all the way back just to see the tip. Unlike the worn pyramids he'd seen in photos, this one's tip was gilded in gold, with fresh black and ruby hieroglyphs painted on the smooth facade. He wondered if they had actually looked like this when they'd been built.

But he wasn't wondering at the architecture for very long, because the moment they reached the base, twin torches burst into flame ahead of them. That's when he realized the darker shadow there was in fact a tunnel.

Torch after torch illuminated deeper within the tunnel, just enough to see a few feet ahead.

They careened toward the entry, not slowing down one bit.

It didn't seem wide or tall enough for them to fit.

Cody reached out and grabbed the dashboard on instinct, bracing for impact.

"Look out!" Jayson yelled to no one.

But the buggy bolted through the opening, just missing the sides by an inch. Cody found himself hunching down, then straightened himself up with a half-hearted giggle.

The buggy bounced and swayed as it raced down the tunnel. Cody's heart firmly lodged itself in his throat. They weren't on any tracks that he could see. At any second he expected the buggy to veer off course. If it shifted by even an inch on either side, they would crash.

"Yaaaasss!" Jayson yelled out. Then his cheer turned into a yelp.

Cody looked over to see Jayson peeling cobwebs off his face and out of his mouth.

Inga giggled behind them.

"See?" she said. "Spiders."

"What?" Jayson asked. "Where? I *hate* spiders."

He jerked and looked around.

And in the process, he bumped the steering wheel.

For a split second, Cody didn't think anything would happen—after all, this was a ride, and their cart was being guided by the ride's mechanics.

But it was a brief thought, because the moment Jayson touched the steering wheel, the buggy shifted.

"Careful!" Inga screamed.

The buggy's side scraped against the wall, snapping off a side-view mirror.

Jayson jolted and grabbed the wheel, but he overcorrected: The buggy bumped into the other wall, knocking off that mirror, too.

"Hit the brakes!" Cody yelled.

Because just then, the tunnel opened.

Into a narrow bridge stretching across an endless dark chasm.

The buggy screeched and skidded, spun a 180, and came to a breathless stop halfway across the crumbling bridge, its front wheels just narrowly gripping the edge.

"Don't. Move. A muscle," Cody warned.

The three of them sat stock-still, none of them moving, none of them even daring to breathe.

Around them, the torches flickered.

Below them, the deep darkness yawned.

"Should we call out?" Inga whispered. "Maybe this is a glitch?"

"I don't know—" Cody began, but then Jayson screamed.

"Spider!" Jayson yelled.

He jerked to the side, swatting away an enormous brown tarantula.

The spider flew off his shoulder and dropped down into the abyss.

A second passed.

Then the stone beneath them gave way.

The buggy teetered forward, and tumbled down into the darkness.

They screamed.

They screamed until their lungs hurt, but they didn't stop, because the drop didn't stop, either.

They fell for what felt like minutes, *hours*. They fell until Cody thought they would fall right through the center of the earth and out the other side.

And then the realization dawned that they weren't falling anymore.

"Guys," Cody whispered. "What just happened?"

Darkness still surrounded them.

But he could tell they were no longer plummeting to their deaths. They hadn't smashed into the ground—and a fall that far surely should have created a crash landing.

And he realized, too, that he was no longer sitting down, strapped into the buggy's seat.

He was standing.

"Are we . . ." Jayson asked beside him. "Are we dead?"

"*Yes*," boomed a voice.

It wasn't Inga.

The voice was deep and ageless, and the moment it spoke, a dozen torches burst into flame around them, their fires unearthly green and teal.

That torchlight illuminated a huge obsidian statue in front of them.

Anubis.

The jackal-headed lord of the underworld towered three stories tall, its regal skirt in solid gold and its eyes glowing green emeralds. The doglike face glowered down at them. In one hand, the statue held a set of silver scales. An enormous, tufted feather balanced on one end. On the other, three orbs of light glowed a pallid blue.

"You have plummeted to your deaths," the statue boomed. "And your souls have been judged against the feather of Maat. You are bound to stay here in the underworld with me. Unless . . ."

"Unless what?" Cody blurted out. He didn't want to be stuck here.

"Unless you find the Scroll of Thoth," Anubis

said. "Retrieve it for me, and I will let you leave. Fail, and you will stay here for eternity. You have thirty minutes. Starting . . . now!"

The flames around them burst so bright they blinded Cody. When he could see again, they were alone in the cavernous room—the statue of Anubis was nowhere to be seen. Cody's wrist buzzed.

He looked down to find he was still in his explorer clothes, and his watch face now had a countdown timer. Thirty minutes. And counting.

"What just happened?" Jayson repeated. "Was that . . . was that really Anubis?"

Inga started to laugh.

"Don't you see?" she asked.

Jayson shook his head. Even Cody's brain was having a hard time computing what was going on.

"It was all part of the ride. All of it! Pyramid *Plummet*, remember? That was all planned. I bet the ride's creators knew they needed to scare the driver so they'd bump the wheel, and *you* admitted you were scared of spiders, so that's what they chose. We had our plummet, and now we must escape. Just like the park's name! Isn't this exciting?"

For having just fallen an impossible depth into the bowels of the underworld, Inga was absolutely beaming.

"No," Jayson admitted. "No, that wasn't exciting at all. I nearly peed myself."

Cody cackled, and even Jayson grinned sheepishly and started to laugh.

"Come on," Inga said. "I bet we get extra points if we find the scroll before the countdown ends. It looks like there's a tunnel over there."

And before either of them could say anything, she turned and jogged off toward the only tunnel out of here.

"Doesn't she know that's a bad idea?" Jayson said as she disappeared down the hall. "This is how people in movies get split up. I mean—"

But whatever he was about to say was cut off as a stone door slammed down over the entrance, blocking Inga from sight.

Jayson groaned.

"Looks like we're going to split up," Cody said.

"At least *we're* together," Jayson said. "Inga can clearly handle this herself."

The moment the words left his mouth, the floor beneath them rumbled.

A crack split between them, and red light poured out. Along with intense heat that made sweat break over Cody's skin.

Lava.

The floor quickly split and spread, the chasm of lava growing between them.

"Jump!" Cody yelled.

"No way, man. *You* jump! That lava looks hot!"

It did. It gurgled and slurped with a dangerous light. They might have managed to survive the fall, but Cody did *not* want to know what it felt like to fall into that. He already knew how hot the suit could make him from the sun. This would be a million times worse.

"There's an opening behind you!" Cody called out. The space between him and Jayson was a good five feet wide now. "Go find the scroll. It's the only way to win."

"What about you?" Jayson asked.

"I'll be fine. I'm sure—"

Lava spat high up between them, sending sparks raining to the floor. Cody leaped back. When he glanced behind himself, though, he realized there was no door on his side.

Just a crescent of floor that was very quickly sliding into the wall. If he didn't act soon, he'd be trapped.

And then the lava would claim him.

17

"Come on, you have to jump!" Jayson yelled.

Cody considered. Maybe there was a secret passageway on his side of the gap. Maybe there was another way out.

But he didn't see anything on his side, and the gap grew wider as the lava bubbled higher.

He wasn't very athletic. He would never make the jump.

He didn't have a choice.

It was now or never.

He took a few steps back. Took a deep breath.

And ran.

He leaped high over the bubbling lava, the heat scorching him as he soared. He was also yelling at the top of his lungs, maybe in excitement, probably in fear. The leap seemed to take impossibly long. He wasn't going to make it.

He wasn't going to make it.

But then he landed.

Right on the edge.

He teetered backward.

And Jayson's quick hands grabbed him, yanking him to safety. Cody practically tumbled on top of his new friend.

"Thank you," Cody gasped. "I thought I was going to die."

"Not on my watch," Jayson said. "Come on. Let's find this thing before Inga does."

Together, they jogged toward the tunnel, the lava bubbling away behind them.

"That was sick," Jayson said as they turned down another passage. "I swear you soared like five feet high."

Cody laughed. "I think you're exaggerating."

"Me? Never."

They'd walked down a few different tunnels, but very little had changed. The lava was far behind them, and now that it was out of sight, the fear that had coursed through Cody's veins turned to pure adrenaline.

They'd crashed a buggy and plummeted to the

underworld and he'd just leaped over *real* lava. Well, maybe not real, but it *felt* real.

This.

Was.

Awesome.

The air grew colder and heavier, dusty and dry. Oppressive.

And it wasn't just that—the tunnel was getting narrower.

"Ummm," Jayson mumbled as Cody started walking in front—it was too narrow to go side by side anymore. "I don't like this. I'm kind of claustrophobic."

Cody glanced over his shoulder. "And the game knows," he said. "Come on, I think I see something up ahead."

And it was true. Something was glinting in the darkness far in front of him. Something golden.

He wondered if it was the scroll.

Except . . .

After a few more steps, it was clear the tunnel wasn't going to get any wider. It had narrowed so much that Cody was going to have to shuffle sideways if he wanted to go any farther.

"I *really* don't like this," Jayson said behind him. "Maybe we should turn around."

"There's nothing back there," Cody reminded him. "Besides, this is a theme park, remember. This is all orchestrated, and we're all under observation. Nothing bad is going to happen here."

"Says the guy who was nearly swallowed up by lava."

"It's just a game," Cody said. "Come on. I'll lead and talk you through it. I think the passage opens a few feet ahead. We'll get the scroll and get out of here and I'll buy you a milkshake."

"Everything is free here!" Jayson yelped.

Cody just laughed. "I had to try something. Fine. I'll buy you a milkshake when we've left the park. But only if you stop whining. Deal?"

It hit him then that he was telling an international pop star to stop whining, *and* he was promising to buy him a shake. Jayson Torn, who could probably afford like a billion shakes if he wanted.

But Jayson just laughed and agreed to the deal.

"Just . . . keep talking, okay? About anything other than being buried underground."

"Okay," Cody said, squeezing farther into the tunnel. The walls were getting tighter. He didn't want to admit it, but even *he* was starting to freak out a little bit. *It's just a game, it's just a game*, he tried to remind himself. It didn't really help. "Tell me about, I don't know, the coolest place you've been."

"Well," Jayson said. He shuffled slowly behind him. Cody could tell that Jayson was trying not to panic. His breath was fast and his voice was strained.

But at least he was still moving. "Last winter, I disappeared to this tiny village in Iceland for a few weeks. Only my parents and manager knew. Totally off the radar. At night, I could see the northern lights from the hot tub—did you know they have geothermal hot tubs *outside* there? It was so unreal. But then we got a huge storm, and the wind and snow didn't stop for like three days straight."

"That sounds so cool," Cody said. He let himself envision it—the bitter winds, the sweeping snow, the northern lights. It sounded magical. He'd never done anything even remotely that fun. He kept moving forward. The passage was starting to widen out again. And, yes! There was *definitely* a treasure of some sort glittering in the distance. "Maybe next year we can go together."

Jayson didn't respond.

Cody made it a few more feet, and the tunnel widened. Enough for him to finally walk the right way. He looked behind him to call out to Jayson and encourage him on.

But when he looked into the shadows of that twisting, winding tunnel, Jayson was nowhere to be seen.

"Jayson? Jayson!" Cody called out.

But his voice echoed in emptiness. Jayson was gone.

Cody wanted to go back in and find him, but his watch buzzed.

Ten minutes remained. How had they already spent twenty minutes down here?

It was enough to remind him that this was a game, and he still had a job to do. Jayson would be okay. They couldn't be hurt. Right?

He looked back to the treasure. Maybe a hundred feet away, on a pedestal of stone, he saw it. That golden *something* that had to be the scroll. Jayson would forgive him if he continued on with the game. After all, if he won, they'd all be released and able to move on to the next ride. And get that milkshake.

"Okay," he whispered to himself. "Let's do this."

He walked toward the golden light.

Darkness seeped around him. He couldn't see where he was putting his feet. All he knew was that the tunnel was wider here. All he knew was that he was getting closer. He was almost there.

Then he set his foot down, and his foot kept going.

He windmilled his arms and jumped backward just in time to keep from falling.

Into a pit.

A pit of scorpions.

Black, glistening shadows scuttled atop one another with the sound of rattling fingernails. Beady little eyes and sharp tails flickered in the darkness. Just seeing them made his skin crawl.

He didn't want to know how it would feel to be down there, with them scuttling atop him, their tiny pincers and needle feet and sharp tails poking through the thin fabric of his outfit . . .

It took a moment for him to realize that there were pedestals stretched out across the expanse of scorpions. Too far apart to walk, but just close enough to jump. Almost.

"You've already done this once," he told himself. "You can do it again."

He looked to the glittering treasure at the end of the tunnel, just beyond the scorpion pit. He bit his lip. Made up his mind.

Cody took a few steps back. Forced down his doubts. And ran.

He soared over the space, the scorpions practically reaching up to pull him down. His foot landed on the first stone. Carried him over to the second. And the third.

He was going to make it. He was going to—

Something sharp stabbed into his heel on the final pedestal. He stumbled, heart leaping to his throat as he toppled toward the scorpion pit, everything in slow motion as he felt his end coming for him . . .

But momentum kept him moving forward, and even though he'd stumbled, he managed to close the gap on the last leap. He made it across the pit with a thud, scrambling the last bit of the way to be clear of the scorpions clicking and threatening behind him. He lay there momentarily, gasping with exhilaration and fear. Then another pulse of pain in his ankle made him glance down.

Had he twisted his ankle on the landing?

He pushed himself to sitting and pulled up the leg of his suit.

And there, red and blistering on his skin, was a welt ringed in purple veins.

"Oh no," he whispered.

He looked at the pit.

To the single scorpion sitting on the final pedestal, pincers open and tail ready.

He'd been stung.

19

Panic raced through Cody's veins, and distantly he knew that that was a bad thing, because the faster his pulse went, the faster the poison would spread. But the moment he thought *that*, his fear doubled, and his heartbeat along with it.

No, no. It was okay. It was all part of the game. They weren't real scorpions and this wasn't a real sting. His suit was just, like, causing a pain response or something. Nothing real or dangerous. It was just a game.

Just a game.

He pushed himself up to standing, swaying slightly from what he hoped was adrenaline and not venom. He put a hand on the wall to steady himself. His ankle throbbed.

Ahead, the golden treasure awaited.

Slowly, making sure he wasn't about to fall into a pit of cobras or trigger a spike trap, he made his way to the end of the hall. Even though his head was feeling woozy and his eyes were a little cloudy and his ankle felt worse, excitement welled within him.

He had found the scroll. With seven minutes left to spare.

He had found the scroll, and that would endear him to Inga and Jayson even more.

He just had to reach it.

He just had—

He stumbled.

Fell onto his hands and knees.

He looked up to the scroll. To the glimmering, golden scroll on its pedestal, only a dozen feet away.

He tried to get up again, but pain lanced through him. He cried out.

"Help!" he called. "I think something's wrong. I've been injured!"

Silence answered.

He continued pulling himself forward.

Maybe if he got the scroll, if he ended the game . . .

The room was going dark.

His head was foggier than ever.

He couldn't keep his eyes open.

He wasn't going to make it.

"Please," he mumbled. "Somebody. Help me."

He looked up to the scroll.

Blinked.

The jackal-headed Anubis was in front of him.

"You have been judged, Cody Baxter," the statue said, holding up its scales. "And there is no help for you here."

Anubis chuckled.

Darkness pulled Cody down.

And right before the world blanked out, he realized that Anubis sounded a lot like Mr. Gould.

"Dude, what was that?"

Jayson's voice broke through the haze. Darkness ebbed away, replaced with antiseptic scents and harsh white lights. Cody winced. He almost preferred the darkness.

"What?" Cody mumbled. He rolled over. Wait, why was he in a bed? Where was he?

He asked that, along with "Did we win?"

Jayson smiled. He was sitting on a chair beside what Cody was quickly learning was a hospital bed.

"Yeah, man, we won." He reached over and tapped Cody's watch. Cody looked down. His vision was still blurry, but fireworks were exploding over the screen, along with the numbers 238. "I got two fifty. Inga got a perfect three hundred—she got to the scroll first and found you there, passed out. Apparently we were scored on individual performance."

His grin faded.

"The real question, though, is why did you collapse? We had to take you to the infirmary. You looked pretty bad."

Cody looked around.

If this was an infirmary, it was the strangest one he'd ever seen.

Every wall was silver, their surfaces so smooth he could see his reflection staring back a hundredfold in them. Harsh white lights beamed down from overhead, and in every corner was a tiny black camera. Save for him and Jayson, there didn't seem to be another living soul in here. Where was the doctor?

"I was stung," Cody said. "By a scorpion."

He glanced down to his legs, but the sheets covered everything. And when he flexed his foot, even though he felt a little ache, the sharp pain from before was gone.

"That's impossible, though," Jayson said. "Those weren't real scorpions. They were just holograms. Just like the pit and the tunnel and all that. None of it could really hurt you. Right?" His voice hitched a little bit, like he was scared of the answer.

Cody just shrugged. It sure *felt* real.

"It doesn't make any sense," Cody said. "Maybe I was just stressed out or something?"

Jayson's eyebrows furrowed.

"Maybe," he said. "Maybe."

A door in one of the smooth, mirrored walls slid open. It wasn't a nurse that stepped out, but a robot. It looked vaguely humanoid, all smooth and white and chrome, with comforting glowing blue eyes. Though its lack of a mouth made it look like an alien.

"He's all better," Jayson said. "But you still haven't said what caused it."

"Stress," replied the robo-doc. Its metallic voice conveyed no emotion. "You are free to go. We suggest rest and plenty of fluids."

"Do they ever suggest anything else?" Jayson mumbled.

The robot gestured to the door, a clear sign that it was time for them to leave. Which was fine by Cody—this room was giving him the creeps. He'd known they were all under surveillance, but this was the first time he truly felt it. Like a lab rat.

As he stood, his leg twinged again.

"You okay?" Jayson asked, noticing Cody wince.

"Yeah, fine," Cody replied. He tried not to hobble as he made his way to the door.

He glanced over his shoulder and looked at one of the cameras.

It was then he remembered his final moments in the pyramid. The towering statue of Anubis speaking with Mr. Gould's tongue.

There is no help for you here, he'd said.

Cody tried to convince himself that it had just been his imagination. But as he made his way into the early evening sun, he couldn't help but feel like the statue had been telling the truth.

They went to meet Inga in the space-themed part of the park. Gone were the pyramids and heat and dust. Here, everything was gleaming silver and crystalline lights. Tiny orbs floated overhead as Cody and Jayson made their way down the boulevard, while constellations and planets swirled impossibly underfoot. Trees has been replaced with silvery alien plants with glowing blue and purple foliage that waved at them as they passed. Robots buzzed around their legs, all apparently on some very important mission. Even the sky here was changed. The air above them was dark blue and filled with glimmering stars, the Milky Way a brilliant white ribbon through the cosmos.

"Is she doing a ride without us?" Cody asked, looking around at all the attractions. Big Dipper Disaster and Intergalactic Terror and Orion Races were just a few of the dozens of rides they passed, their names blazing brilliant blue neon.

"Nah, she's in the Space Dust Diner. I may or

may not have told her you owed me a milkshake." Jayson grinned and pointed toward a giant silver flying saucer that somehow hovered a few feet off the ground. A paper-thin silver ramp led from its hatch. It didn't look strong enough to support a small dog, but as Cody watched, a couple kids strolled down it. It was then he realized that their explorer uniforms had once more been transformed. Everyone here wore a glittering silver space suit, including him and Jayson. Tiny blue lights raced across the suits, almost like veins.

"Whoa," Cody muttered. "These are amazing."

"Right?" Jayson said. They started up the ramp and into the diner. "I've worked with some amazing costume designers, but none of them could pull this off. I wonder if we'll ever stop being surprised?"

"I hope not," Cody said. Then they were inside, and he saw Inga waving at them from a corner booth. Her smile made him blush.

"Hello, boys!" she called out.

Cody and Jayson sat down across from her. Even the seats of the booth were space themed, with a glimmering black fabric pockmarked with glowing silver stars. "I've just ordered. But I bet you could get your order in soon so we can eat together." She looked at Cody, and he felt his throat constrict. "How are you feeling?"

"I'm okay," he managed.

"What happened?"

"Overexcitement," Cody said. He felt bad for lying, but he didn't want to try and explain it to her when he wasn't certain. As always, he wanted to shift the attention away from himself. "Where's the menu?"

"It's so cool," Inga said. "Check your watch."

Cody did so, and the word *menu* appeared on-screen. He tapped it; the next moment, comets shot up from the table. In the glittering dust of their tails, the menu appeared in a spinning, sparkling hologram.

"Whoa," Cody said for what felt like the millionth time that day. Everything was from his dream list of favorite foods.

"The menus are totally custom," Inga explained. "Your menu is different from mine, and it's catered to what your body is craving or needing right now."

It seemed like magic. Everything that he could possibly want in that moment was on display. Which almost made it harder to choose, seeing as there were nearly a dozen amazing choices, when he was used to having only one or two.

"How do I order?" he asked.

"By deciding," she said. "I think the tracker thing we got monitors our thoughts or something."

The idea was a bit scary, but he decided to just go with it; he settled on a slice of pizza, a side order of cheesy fries, and a chocolate-peanut-butter milk-shake. The moment he made the mental decision, the menu vanished in a flurry of sparks.

When his and Jayson's menus disappeared, he looked around at the café.

The place was pretty big, with multiple levels and floating asteroids and little robot UFOs darting around, delivering food to the upper floors. There were maybe five or six other kids in there with them. The floors and walls were translucent, so it seemed like everyone was floating in the neon darkness of space. One group of kids was huddled together tightly. They seemed to be comforting the young boy in the middle—Cody vaguely recognized him as some social media influencer—who appeared to be crying. What was there to cry about here? Maybe he missed home?

That's also when he noticed the scoreboard on the side of the wall.

It spanned two stories, and even though he couldn't read the fine print, he could see the gist: Everyone had been ranked based on how many games they'd played and how well they'd done. He couldn't see himself up there, but it began cycling through the top five, show-ing their faces and scores and their top games.

Meg-A was number one.

For some reason, that made Cody's guts squirm.

He hated seeing someone who was so rude doing so well. It didn't seem fair.

It also didn't seem like he was anywhere near the top of that list. Meg-A's score was close to a thousand.

"Don't worry about it," Jayson said, clearly noticing Cody's dismay. "It's just a number."

But Mr. Gould had promised a special prize for the winner, and a part of Cody really wanted to win that prize. To prove that he hadn't just gotten here from luck, but because he was supposed to be here. Because he'd earned it.

He realized he didn't want to just prove it to everyone else—he wanted to prove it to himself.

"Are you sure you're okay?" Inga asked again. "You look a little sick still."

"Totally fine," Cody said. He realized he'd been scowling while looking at the screen. "The doctor said nothing was wrong with me."

Except for the fact that I'm pretty certain I was actually stung by a scorpion and I swear I heard Mr. Gould threatening me. But he didn't say that. Of course he didn't—they'd think he was losing it.

"The *robot* doctor," Jayson amended. "Mr. Gould wasn't kidding when he said no adults were allowed in here! I bet the robots do everything."

Inga's brow furrowed in concern.

"That is a mildly troubling thought. What if we need their help?"

There is no help for you here.

Before he could voice his worry, their food arrived on the backs of tiny UFOs. No one spoke for the next few minutes, save for making happy noises over their food. It was good. *Really* good. Cody hadn't tasted a shake so sweet or food so savory ever. The fries were perfectly crisp and the pizza perfectly greasy and the shake was better than anything he'd ever had, and in those moments it was easy to forget his sadness and the strange occurrence of being stung.

Then Jayson started talking, and that happiness melted away a bit.

"So, my man," Jayson said, "tell us about yourself."

Cody nearly choked on his bite of burger.

"What?"

"You know. Where are you from? What do you do? That sort of thing."

The truth was, Cody didn't know what to say. He'd wanted to come here to reinvent himself, which meant lying. But he'd already promised himself that he wouldn't try to be anything other than what he was around these two—especially after Jayson had blindly defended him. On the other hand, if they learned how boring his life actually was, they might not want to stick around him.

Maybe if he bent the truth a little bit, it would be okay. Embellish.

"I'm from the middle of nowhere," Cody said, which was true. No one had heard of his town, and there was no point pretending otherwise. Especially since he knew that Jayson had read his brief bio in the newsletter. "But I travel all the time. My parents are both investment bankers, so we get to go on some rad vacations."

"Where have you gone?" Inga asked.

Panic raced through him, but Cody had prepared for this, too. Shamed as he was to admit it, he'd spent weeks preparing cover stories and researching exotic locales. Just on the off chance he got into ESCAPE. Just in case he needed to pretend to be something he was not.

He kept his cool and continued his cover story.

"Mostly tropical places," he said. "Thailand and Cambodia and the like. My mom likes beaches and my dad likes being off grid, so we find these little resorts no one's heard about and where no one can find us."

"That sounds lovely," Inga said dreamily, her own milkshake forgotten. "I would love to find places like that."

"Me too," Jayson said. He punched Cody on the shoulder. "Hey! Maybe when we get out of here we can all go on vacation together."

Another jolt of fear ran through Cody. He'd

forgotten that to stay friends with them he'd need to continue his cover story *after*.

"Maybe," Cody said. "We're pretty busy now. I'm in a band and we're starting to do a local tour."

"What?!" Jayson yelped. "Why didn't you say something? We could collaborate. What do you play?"

"Tenor sax," Cody said. Another half-truth. Yes, he played saxophone. He was even pretty good at it—first chair. But the only band he'd ever been in was the school one, and the only tour it did was for holiday concerts and the like.

Still, his pulse was racing. Even if he played sax, there was no way he was good enough to play while Inga and Jayson sung.

The two of them seemed to be really into the idea, though—immediately they started jabbering about different musical trends and how sax solos were making a comeback and maybe they could do some sort of retro-synth-pop-ballad and . . .

Cody had to stop listening. It made his head spin, and not with excitement.

He could be in a music video with Inga and Jayson, two of the biggest teen names in music right now.

And that would prove to the world that he was nothing but a fake.

They decided to do something a little more low-key after dinner. They skipped the rides proclaiming daring escapes or races or anything dangerous, supposedly because they were full—though Cody noticed both Inga and Jayson looking at him worriedly. Cody didn't mention his hurting ankle again, though he did have to force himself to keep from looking at it. He still hadn't peeled back the suit to see if there was a puncture wound underneath.

He didn't want to know.

"We can totally do something more exciting," Cody said. "Want to do the Saturn Spinners?"

Jayson's eyes bulged. He'd eaten twice what Cody had.

"Let's stick to something a little calmer."

"Like this one?" Inga suggested, pointing to the ride beside her.

Cosmic Cruise.

That didn't sound too bad.

Once more, there wasn't a line for this ride. They walked through the empty queue, this one a tunnel roped with neon lights. The walls and floor and ceiling were all glass panels looking out into an impossible solar system—galaxies swirled and stars winked and comets whizzed past. It felt like traveling within the deepest part of space. Cody had to hold on to the neon banister to keep from falling over—when he looked up at the swirling constellations, he was hit with the strongest sense of vertigo. He could have spent hours just walking around, staring at all the scenery and marveling at how it was all done.

Could have. But then he'd lose the games, and there was no way he'd leave here without winning.

Inga turned her interrogation to Jayson as they walked down the long corridor toward the ride's entrance.

"Why did you decide to come here?" she asked.

Cody looked over to Jayson, watching his face closely. If Cody hadn't been looking, he might have missed the expression that came over Jayson's face.

He knew that expression well—the slight furrow of his forehead that came when he himself was about to lie.

"Just wanted a new adventure," he said. "Touring and all that gets boring after a while. Thought it would be cool to do something not related to music, you know?"

Inga nodded. "It *is* nice to not be thinking about it all day."

"And yet you're talking about it," Cody said with a wry smile.

"Well, we talk about what we love. Even if we hate it at times."

They reached the front of the empty line and faced a large round hatch in the side of a shiny silver wall. The air in here was cool, the lights flickering and dazzling. And when a series of wheels and gears spun on the hatch, releasing a billow of cold fog that settled around their feet, Cody felt like he was walking into a different dimension.

Multicolored lights flickered behind the obscuring mist.

"Welcome to the adventure of a lifetime," came a robotic yet soothing female voice. "Please step inside. Our journey is about to begin."

The trio looked at one another. It was plain that

they were all wondering the same thing: *What is this going to entail?*

They didn't bother asking.

"At least there aren't any scorpions in space," Jayson said, grinning at Cody.

"Let's hope," Cody replied.

They stepped inside.

22

If this had been any other park, Cody would have expected some sort of spacecraft simulator. There would be blinking control panels and uncomfortable pleather seats and tiny screens showing pixelated galaxies. Jerky motors would jolt the capsule around in a poor imitation of space flight while crackly music and bad sound effects would blare from old speakers. At least, that's what he would have expected at a normal theme park. This, of course, was different.

It felt like walking into the lobby of a beautiful, high-end hotel. Not at all a metallic, lifeless vessel. Great palm plants sat in silver vases and rich red carpet spread out before them. A huge crystalline fountain in the shape of a star bubbled in front of them. The lobby was easily the size of a football field, or maybe even bigger. It was hard to tell with all the columns arching up past the balconies. Cody followed them up with his gaze.

His jaw dropped open.

Because there, arched like the ceiling of some old cathedral, were glass panes that revealed the literal heavens. Stars and galaxies swirled beautifully beyond the glass, revealing a world that nearly made tears come to his eyes.

"It's beautiful," Inga whispered. She stood so close to Cody that their arms lightly touched. His skin seemed to tingle with electricity beneath his suit. "I had been worried . . . One of my fears is being stranded in space. Which is silly, since I have no desire to be an astronaut. But being lost out there, all alone. Well, I suppose it isn't as scary as it might be. This is quite stunning."

He wanted to reach out and take her hand, but the moment was interrupted by the arrival of a robot.

"Welcome, travelers," said the robotic greeter.

The robot was an android with metallic skin, wearing a crisp black flight attendant uniform trimmed in silver and azure. She wore a tiny hat angled to the side, and her hair was made of silver strands. Her eyes glowed as blue as the trim of her jacket.

"My name is Cassiopeia," she said. "And I am your guide for this cruise. First, I must ask, what sort of adventure would you like on your cruise tonight?"

"Something relaxing," Jayson piped in immediately.

"Yes," Inga said. "Perhaps something educational?"

"Very well," Cassiopeia said. "Perhaps I might interest you in an intergalactic raft ride? Nothing could be more relaxing than rafting down the Milky Way in our totally secure space pods. I could also bring you to the observatory deck, where you could watch our travels in complete comfort, if you would like something even slower paced."

"Rafting sounds kind of fun," Jayson admitted. He looked to Cassiopeia. "You're sure there aren't any, like, space sharks or something?"

The android smiled.

"No space sharks. Just tranquility. Here on the Cosmic Cruise, your relaxation is our premier destination."

Cassiopeia wasn't lying.

She guided the three of them past the main foyer and down a long hallway lined with moving photos of solar systems and galaxies, each of them as beautiful as a painting. At least, Cody thought they were photos. On closer look, it almost seemed like they were looking outside.

At the end of the hall was a smaller room filled with lush white sand. The air in there was warmer, and a tropical breeze wafted over the dunes. For a split second Cody considered turning around—he'd had more than enough sand for one lifetime, and he could just imagine little space scorpions burrowing about. Except this was lush and vibrant, nothing at all like the harsh and desolate pyramid. A lazy river twisted from one end of the room to the other, each end disappearing through a swirling portal of mist and rainbow lights.

Outside the glass walls, Cody could see the river continuing out and floating through the cosmos. Out there, the river twinkled with stars and danced alongside the Milky Way. He had to bite back another gasp of awe.

"Here we are," Cassiopeia said pleasantly. She gestured to the three small rafts nestled on the banks, right beside the sparkling river. They were bright yellow and rubber, with a small silver box in the front covered in knobs and levers. Some sort of control console?

"Your rafts are completely automated and equipped with the latest in life-support technologies. You will be able to speak to one another as if you are on a normal rafting trip, and not billions of light-years away from home or oxygen." She smiled warmly as she said it. It was almost unnerving, the sweetness, but Cody tried not to pay it any mind. It felt a little too close to her saying *What could possibly go wrong?* right before the alarms went off. *It's just a ride—we aren't in space, and there isn't a risk of losing oxygen!*

"The ride is approximately thirty minutes long," she continued. "Although fully automated, you will be able to further control your raft through the console. Should you need a longer or shorter trip, or should you desire a little excitement, you can change it all there.

"Now, passengers, please take to your rafts. The ride is about to begin."

With a somewhat nervous look, Cody and his friends got on their rafts. The material felt just like a normal rubber raft, and the water smelled like salt water. Cassiopeia came over and gave them each a gentle push, guiding them into the river.

"Enjoy your trip," she said. "And be sure to remember—relax!"

Cody's raft gently bumped into Jayson's, which in turn bumped into Inga's. They all giggled. Jayson grabbed on to the ropes looped around Cody's and Inga's rafts, holding them together.

"Just another normal night," Jayson said with a smile.

Then they neared the glowing, fog-filled portal, and the ship washed away in a blanket of pearlescent white.

The Cosmic Cruise was, well, otherworldly.

The moment they were out the gate, they found themselves drifting peacefully atop the Milky Way, stars glinting distantly all around them. Cody turned back to look at the spaceship; it was huge and sleek, all polished steel and blinking lights and windows revealing empty rooms. The park was nowhere to be seen. It truly felt like they were light-years away from Earth.

"This is really cool," Jayson said. He trailed his fingers in the glittering waters below them, his fingers pulling up sparks like sprays of water.

"Yeah," Cody said. He dipped his hand into the water as well. It was warm and fizzed around his fingers like static, sparkling magically.

He knew, of course, that the Milky Way wasn't

really a river running through the cosmos, but a string of galaxies bigger than he could begin to imagine. He knew as well that this wasn't truly a ride through outer space. Both those truths seemed harder to believe the farther along they went.

Everything around them sparkled and swirled, from the celestial waters below them to the stars spread out above.

"This is strange," Inga said.

"What? The fact that we're like literally floating through space on a raft?"

"Well, yes. But no." She fidgeted with something on her raft, by the small control console. She lifted something up. It looked like a toy laser gun. "Why would we need lasers for a relaxing cruise?"

Jayson leaned forward and rummaged around in his own console, pulling out a similar laser. "Well, she did say we could add a little extra excitement, didn't she?"

"I don't think I want any extra excitement." Inga looked nervously to the vastness around them, and Cody remembered her mentioning her fear of being lost in space.

"It's okay," Cody assured her. "We're on easy mode. Tranquil! Remember? We're supposed to be relaxing, not panicking. Nothing bad—"

"Don't you *dare* say nothing bad can happen!"

Jayson yelped. His voice actually squeaked. "That's always when—"

An enormous laser beam blasted right in front of them, sending a huge spray of water and sparks over their rafts. The river in front of them disintegrated, and the rafts rocked treacherously with the waves.

"What in the world was that?" Inga yelled out. She gripped both sides of her raft tightly.

Her laser floated just out of her reach in the water. It bobbed once, then disappeared below and drifted through space.

Cody started trying to paddle over to her spinning raft, while Jayson looked around nervously, holding his laser in shaking hands.

"Did you see anything?" Jayson asked. "Where did it go? Was it an enemy ship?"

Cody glanced up once, but he didn't see anything. Just empty space.

"Just hold on," he tried to tell Inga comfortingly. "I'll be right there." He was only a few feet away . . .

Then another laser blasted right in between them.

The river exploded.

Dissolved.

Inga let out a terrified scream as her raft flew from the river and spiraled into space.

"Inga!" Cody yelled out.

"Cody!" she screamed back.

The river around him and Jayson completely dissolved, sending both of them drifting off in the opposite direction. There was no more water to paddle against.

No way to reach her.

And as he watched Inga drift farther and farther away, he realized the game had made her worst fears come to life.

"We have to help her!" Cody called to Jayson.

"Let us out!" Jayson yelled. "Something's wrong with the ride! Let us out!"

But just like in the pyramid, there was no response. No one came to rescue them.

The simulation didn't end.

If anything, it just felt more real.

And their troubles were only just beginning.

As Cody managed to latch on to Jayson's raft, something flew past them at breakneck speed, so fast it was just a gray streak in the air.

"What—" Jayson began, but another laser fired right beside their joined rafts cut him off.

Cody held on with all his might.

Jayson fired wildly into the ether. The laser beam was bright blue and made a laughable *pew pew* noise when it fired.

Laughable, except Cody didn't think it would be any use against the ship that was targeting them.

"We have to get to Inga," Cody said.

"How?" Jayson yelled. He took aim and fired again. Judging by the return laser shot from the enemy ship, he missed.

"Cassiopeia mentioned something about the control panel. Maybe we can steer."

Jayson nodded. "I'll hold them off. You navigate. But step aside, I'm coming aboard."

With that, Jayson shimmied over to Cody's raft. Which was probably wise, since there was no way Cody could hold the rafts together *and* steer at the same time. But the raft was definitely crowded.

Thankfully, the control console was intuitive: a

steering wheel and a lever to control speed. As well as a few buttons he was scared to try.

"Ready?" Cody asked.

"Ready!" Jayson yelled.

Cody thrust the lever forward, and the raft rocketed into space.

Now that they weren't on the calm, crystalline waters of the Milky Way, the ride was choppy and brutal. Cody's teeth chattered in his head while they made their bumpy way through space. He could just barely make out Inga's raft ahead of them, the faintest white spark.

But it wasn't easy.

Because the moment they were on her tail, the enemy ship was on theirs.

Lasers fired all around them. Some from Jayson, some from the ship. Cody swerved left and right and up and down, trying to avoid getting blasted from space.

"Keep it steady!" Jayson yelled. "I can't aim!"

"I can't keep it steady! If I do, we'll get blasted!"

Jayson fired a few shots at the enemy ship. Cody looked over his shoulder, briefly, to see a monstrous cruiser with spiked wings and vicious lights. He could see the helmeted aliens inside their command center. There was no way Cody and his raft could defeat that.

Jayson fired again. It struck, but bounced right off the ship's window.

"Ugh!" he yelled. "It's no use! These are worthless!"

But Cody had an idea.

"Hang on tight!" he said.

And veered right. Hard.

Jayson was flung to the raft and Cody gritted his teeth. This was a horrible idea. But it was the only way to win.

Ahead of them, rocketing through the dark, was an asteroid belt. The giant cruiser would be no good in there, but Cody's tiny raft might just stand a chance.

The cruiser clearly caught on. The ship pummeled Cody's raft with lasers, but he managed to dodge every one.

"Almost there, almost there . . ."

Another laser fired.

This one hit.

Cody yelped as the raft spun out of control.

Jayson screamed as he was tossed from the raft.

"Jayson!" Cody yelled out. "No!"

He raised his arms in futile defense as the raft crashed headfirst into a meteor.

"What in the *nebula* have you done?"

Cassiopeia's voice cut through Cody's own scream.

Cody lowered his own hands and blinked. White light flickered around him. One moment he was in a white room. The next, in the loading bay of where he'd first gotten on the raft. White light flashed, flickered like a bad bulb; the room disappeared. Then, with an almost audible whir, the ship was back.

Cody was still in his raft, and Jayson was sprawled on the sand beside him. Inga stood beside her raft a little farther off, looking terrified and confused.

"What have we done?" Cody asked. He struggled to standing. A huge gash had torn open the front of his raft, and the deflated mess tangled his feet. "What just happened?"

The android strode forward, and her kind eyes became stern.

"You naughty children destroyed park property," she said, pointing to the deflated raft at Cody's feet. "Out. Out!"

"But we didn't do anything!" Jayson yelled.

"Yes," Inga cut in. "That was supposed to be a relaxing ride. We did not ask to be attacked and flung into space!"

The android shook her head.

"You humans and your silly imaginations. No such thing happened. You were in your rafts and then *one of you*"—she glared at Jayson as she said this— "decided to start firing your laser gun. Which was meant for use strictly in emergencies."

"How was that not an emergency?" Cody asked. "We were attacked by an enemy ship. It's still out there!"

"No such thing happened," Cassiopeia said. "I have been monitoring your trip from here." She gestured to the large windows overlooking the Milky Way. And, sure enough, there were no missing chunks from the river, no darting, dangerous enemy ships. "*Why* you decided to then go off course and catapult into the meteor storm, I will not even try to guess. Had I not ended the simulation when I did, you would have caused even more harm to the raft."

"The raft? What about us?" Inga demanded.

Cassiopeia ignored her. "Even though there are no adults in ESCAPE, we *expect* you to be on your best behavior. Otherwise you will be ejected."

Jayson balled his fists and took a step forward, and Cody knew he was about to say something they'd all regret. So he put a hand on Jayson's shoulder.

"Come on," Cody said. "Let's go."

He looked to the android.

"We're sorry," he said. Even though he didn't mean it.

"Sorry?" Jayson spluttered. Cody shook his head and started dragging Jayson away. Inga followed.

"What should we have to be sorry about?" Jayson asked. "That game almost *killed* us."

"I was terrified," Inga whispered. "Even though I knew it was a ride, even though I knew it couldn't hurt me, I was still so scared." She looked pleadingly at Cody. "But it couldn't have hurt us, could it? Not really?"

Jayson looked at Cody. They were in the main entry now, and walking fast. Cody wanted to be as far away from here as possible.

"What happened to you earlier . . ." Jayson whispered. "What if you were really poisoned? What if the danger is real?"

"Poisoned?" Inga asked.

Cody bit his lip. "I sort of lied earlier. I wasn't just exhausted. I was stung when we split up."

"Why didn't you say anything?"

"Because I didn't think it could be real."

"It can't be," Jayson said. "They would never allow something like live scorpions in a theme park. Just like they wouldn't actually let us get killed in outer space. That's impossible. Right?"

Cody didn't have an answer.

At ESCAPE, everything was supposed to be possible.

Even, he was beginning to fear, the danger.

They parted ways outside their suites. The buildings sat on the far end of the park, away from all the rides and surrounded by trees. They looked like ornate hotels from the outside—large Roman columns and fancy uplighting and even a red carpet. And more cameras, in the trees, blinking behind the eyes of the statues, just like everywhere else in the park.

But Cody was too anxious to be impressed. He wasn't tired in the slightest, but after their near-death experience in the space simulation, none of them wanted to do another ride.

The one small positive surprise was realizing that both Cody and Jayson were side by side in their suites.

"Did you want to hang out or something?" Jayson asked.

Cody faked a yawn. "Thanks. But I'm pretty beat after all that. See you in the morning?"

Jayson nodded. Truthfully, Cody *did* want to hang out with Jayson. He didn't want to be alone, and he didn't want to miss his chance to really become friends with one of the coolest kids he'd met. But he knew they would just spend the night speculating about what had happened. He didn't have any answers, and he didn't want to overthink things.

Cody went into his room to change into pajamas and get ready for bed. The room was about the size of his bedroom back home, though the bed was huge and ultra comfy, and the wardrobe was sleek and expertly lit. The bathroom was ornate marble. Everything was luxurious. Everything was better than anything he'd ever experienced before. There were even fancy chocolates on the overstuffed pillows.

There weren't any cameras.

But he was numb to it.

He couldn't get excited over the extravagance when his tired brain wouldn't stop churning over everything that had happened. It had seemed so *real*. He couldn't believe it was all just a simulation. Mr. Gould had promised them at the beginning that everything was perfectly safe, that the danger was only *meant* to look real. But what if it was?

Something didn't seem right here. The close calls seemed a little too close.

The virtual reality seemed less virtual and more like real life.

What if Inga *had* nearly gotten lost? Maybe not in deep space, but in some dangerous corner of the park? What if the pyramid ride *had* glitched when they fell? What if the scorpions *had* been real?

All theme parks had bugs, especially on the first day. But could these glitches be deadly?

It was only as he was about to change into pajamas that finally did what he'd been putting off all day: He looked down at his ankle.

Slowly, he peeled back the fabric of his suit.

And there, a bruised red on his flesh, was the undeniable welt of a scorpion sting.

Cody couldn't sleep, not after that.

He tossed and turned in bed, oddly missing his smaller, much less comfortable bed back home. He wanted to call Patrick or Laura—they were levelheaded; they'd know what was going on. He'd have given anything to go over to Patrick's to play video games and just zone out. But he didn't have his phone. He missed his friends back home more than he thought he would.

He drifted in and out of sleep, his thoughts or dreams dotted with wriggling scorpions and catapulting through space. Inga screaming. Jayson screaming.

So much screaming.

He moaned and rolled over.

Then he realized the scream—well, one of them—was coming from outside.

Panic jolted through him. He was up in a heartbeat and ran to the window.

He couldn't believe his eyes.

A kid was running around down there.

A kid whose arms were covered in *fire*.

This can't be happening, Cody thought. He rubbed his eyes and pinched himself. But the kid was still out there, still screaming.

"Someone has to help them," Cody mumbled. He tapped on his watch, trying to find an emergency button. *I thought Mr. Gould said they were watching at all times?*

But before he could find it, a group of robots wheeled out from the bushes.

One sprayed the kid down in a cloud of smoke that instantly put out the blaze. The others wheeled the kid onto a stretcher. The kid was still moaning in pain. Cody thought he saw one of the robots inject something into the kid's arm.

Then they all vanished down the path, disappearing into the dark like a bad dream.

"Something strange happened last night," Cody said.

"You heard about it, too?" Inga asked.

"No, I saw it."

"What are you two talking about?" Jayson asked.

They were in a café in the Prehistoric Paradise section of the park. The tables here were carved from enormous dinosaur teeth, and giant ferns towered around them while small animals and pterodactyls swooped and scuttled. The pterodactyls, at least, were robotic—they were carrying meals in their beaks to the few other kids scattered about.

"Someone was hurt," Inga said.

"Yeah," Cody replied. "I saw them. They were on fire. Like, real fire. Right outside the suites."

Inga shot him a confused look.

"What? No. That was not it at all. I heard some-one was playing some sort of pirate game. Their ship was pulled down by a kraken. They were not seen again."

Cody's eyes widened in shock. *Wait, two kids were hurt? How is that possible?*

"But that can't be possible," Jayson said. "The rides are all supposed to be completely safe. Like, come on—there aren't *real* kraken, and we aren't really by an ocean. It can't be really dangerous."

"So how do you explain the burning kid?" Inga asked him.

"I don't know," Jayson muttered. "Are you sure you weren't dreaming, Cody?"

"I'm positive," Cody said. "I saw them running around with my own eyes. They were screaming."

"So why didn't you try to get help?" came a voice behind them.

Cody's stomach turned to acid before he even looked around. Meg-A.

She stood there flanked by two of her friends, her hands on her hips and a confrontational look on her face.

"I tried," Cody managed. "I tried calling for help but there was no—"

"Yeah, yeah, whatever," she interrupted. "I don't really care. I know you're a scaredy-cat, and that's why I'm here." She looked to her friends, who both smiled cruelly at Cody. "We're challenging you to a duel."

"What?" Jayson asked.

"Yeah," Meg-A replied. "This park is getting boring. We're already beating all you losers." She looked to the scoreboard. Sure enough, Meg-A and her friends took up the top three spots. By quite a lot of points. "While you were all playing kiddie games, we went and took on the toughest games here. And none of *us* were hurt. *I* think it's all just stories—kids are chickening out or don't want to admit they're homesick."

"But I saw—"

"Didn't I already say I don't care?" Meg-A jabbed. "Look, here's the deal. We've only been here a day and we're already bored. We need competition. And, well, although I don't think *any* of you are competition, I really want to rub your faces in our victory." She smiled wickedly. Even Inga looked affronted by the insults. "So, I thought maybe we could up the stakes. The three of you against the three of us. Winner takes all. What do you say?"

"What do you mean, winner takes all?" Inga asked suspiciously.

Meg-A smiled. "I'm glad you asked. The loser has to go off social media for a full year. Totally silent.

Off grid. Save for one final post supporting the winner. And no music drops, either. Total career killer. Not that any of you really *have* careers anymore." She paused, looking between each of them. "Oh. And the winners gets fifty grand from each of the losers. Total. Cash."

Both Inga and Jayson looked aghast. Cody couldn't imagine either of them agreeing to it—after all, he was so far behind, it would be nearly impossible to catch up to Meg-A and her team. Not to mention, he didn't have the same drive as they would. Without any sort of career, going off grid for him would just be, well, another boring year in his normal life.

He was about to say that this was stupid, because that would tank their careers if they lost, and he couldn't afford to pay—and also *had they forgotten that kids were getting hurt?*—but Inga beat him to the punch.

"We will do it," she said.

"Yeah," Jayson added. "You're on."

Cody's mouth dropped open. "We will?"

"Yes," Jayson said. His jaw was clenched as he reached out to take Meg-A's hand. They shook. The ferocity of his eye contact was enough to level mountains.

"Deal. Better start working on your defeat speech,"

Meg-A said. "We officially start after breakfast. Hope you enjoy your last meal."

When she walked away, Cody felt horrible.

"Look, if that was about defending my honor or something—" Cody began. Jayson cut him off.

"It has nothing to do with you," Jayson said.

"I don't have any money if we lose," Cody muttered. "I might have been exaggerating when I said my parents were rich. We haven't even been on a real vacation in years."

"We won't lose," Jayson said. He took a deep breath and shot Cody a grin. "And I'll pay your portion if we do. Retribution for my rash decision, as my grandmother would say."

"But why? Why risk it?"

"Because she deserves to lose," Inga said coldly. She looked to Jayson, who nodded.

"I feel like I'm missing something," Cody said.

"Don't worry about it," Jayson replied. "Just worry about winning. And this amazing breakfast!"

Because at that moment, their meals were delivered by tiny pterodactyls, the trays hanging from their beaks like storks carrying babies.

It was clear from the way that both Inga and Jayson began chowing down that he wouldn't get any further answer from them. So Cody tried to enjoy his breakfast burrito and strawberry milkshake and orange juice. Tried to. But he kept looking over to Meg-A's table, and when he wasn't watching them, he felt her watching him.

Suddenly, his bad dreams and exhaustion and worries of park malfunctions were forgotten.

He had bigger things to worry about. Like how to keep his friends from regretting ever teaming up with him.

28

"If we lose, though—" Cody began, for what felt like the hundredth time.

"We won't lose," Jayson said.

"There are worse things than losing."

"*Inga*," Jayson hissed. "You're not helping Cody's confidence here."

"I'm just saying," Inga continued, "a year off social media might be kind of nice."

"Don't tell me you're thinking of forfeiting," Jayson said. "I can't be the only one who wants to rub this in Meg-A's face. Right?"

"Of course I'm not forfeiting," Inga said. "She was rude to Cody. She has slammed both of us on social media. I will not forgive that. But I think it wise to remember that our lives don't need to revolve around the internet." She gestured to the wild park around them. "Case in point."

They were walking toward their first competitive game. Meg-A and her two friends were ahead of them. Cody never caught their names. Probably because the two girls never gave them. He thought he recognized them, though. One might have been an Instagram model. The other he was pretty certain he'd seen in commercials for tooth whiteners—he thought she was either a celeb's kid or a child star trying to catch her break.

Neither Cody nor his friends mentioned the rumors of injured kids or what Cody had witnessed again. Meg-A's necessary defeat was all-consuming.

Jayson sighed. "Yeah. But I still want to beat her."

"We will," Inga said. She smiled sadly to herself. "And perhaps afterward I will take some time off anyway. This is rather nice. I don't feel quite as stressed as I did before."

"What do you mean?" Cody asked. He couldn't imagine a pop star being stressed. Didn't she have, like, massage therapists and assistants to help with all that?

"I mean the internet can be a terrible place when you are a girl," she said. "Especially a popular one."

A cloud seemed to pass over her usually sunny features.

"I know what you mean," Jayson said. "It's rough out there when you're different."

Inga nodded sadly, and even though Cody was ultimately grateful he'd never had to deal with online harassment like that, he still felt a little envious that the two of them had another thing to bond over.

His thoughts were derailed by Meg-A calling out that she'd picked their first game.

TRIASSIC TERROR

Not exactly the most heartening sign, but Meg-A seemed excited and there was no way he was going to back out and show weakness now. It was all just a game; the glitches were just glitches. The dinosaurs and danger were all manufactured. There was nothing *terrible* inside here. Except for Meg-A and her friends.

The sign was etched in sandstone like all the other rides in this area, though this one had two pterodactyl statues on each end.

It was only when they were nearly under the sign that the creatures *moved*, and he realized they weren't exactly statues after all. The dinosaurs seemed to watch him hungrily as he walked under the sign and into the empty queue. He wondered if there were cameras in their eyes. Rumbling growls echoed from the ferns around them, and small dinosaurs scurried about, rustling the fronds and darting across their feet. Every once in a while, the ground would shake, and he wasn't certain if it was from an earthquake or the distant volcano or, perhaps, some enormous dino out for a meal.

He held back a shiver and wondered if maybe he *should* ask about picking a different game. One a little less scary. Then he looked up at Meg-A and her friends. The moment he saw them, his nerves were replaced with resilience. No matter what, he was going to win this one. For his friends, and for himself. He wasn't about to let himself get scared off over nothing.

"You losers ready?" Meg-A asked when they reached the front of the line.

"Born ready," Cody said. He tried to stand up tall, shoulders back, chin up. He tried to sound more confident than he really was.

"Ladies first, then," Meg-A said, gesturing to the door. This one was two giant stone plinths, thick vines hanging in front of them.

Inga took a step forward, but Cody knew who the insult was for. He ducked his head and stepped past the vines, ahead of his friends and ready for whatever the park would throw at him next.

Cody was not prepared for this.

He stood at the edge of a cliff, the ground thousands of feet below him. Clouds floated past at eye level and the trees below were so distant, they looked like tiny pieces of broccoli. Just like before, there was no sign of the rest of the park. The world stretched on forever, filled with a hazy horizon of trees and tall pillars of stone. And brooding above it all was an active volcano, sparks and plumes of smoke billowing above it, the lava within ready to burst.

Inga and Jayson stood beside him, looking around in wonder. Meg-A and her teammates were nowhere to be seen.

A voice echoed from the heavens, loud and ominous.

"Players. You have thirty minutes to best your opponents and secure your victory. The team that has collected the most rings and reaches the nest when the time is up is the winner. But remember: Every member of your team must reach the nest to be qualified. Succeed as a team, or fail as one."

A great bronze ring the size of a Hula-Hoop appeared in the air before him.

"Bronze rings are common and worth five points." A silver hoop appeared, slightly smaller than the first, maybe the size of a beach ball. "Silver are rarer, and may be guarded. They are worth twenty points." Finally, a gold ring appeared. It was no larger than a bracelet and glinted in the sun. "Gold rings are highly treasured and highly guarded. They are worth two hundred points. But finding them may come with a price."

The rings before him disappeared. But then, in the distant clouds, he saw great bronze rings blink into being, floating in the air like a race course of hoops. Some stayed in place, while others spun or moved up and down slowly. Other shapes appeared as well. Shapes with wings and shrill cries.

Cody's watch buzzed, and he glanced down to see a blinking "30."

"Begin!" the voice called out.

"What do we do?" Jayson asked. He looked

around in confusion. They were hundreds of feet in the air, and there were no ropes or visible way to reach the rings.

Inga grinned.

"I think we just jump," she said.

"But what if it's real?" Cody asked. "What if it's dangerous?"

A hologram appeared in the sky. Meg-A's team had just scored five points.

"Only one way to find out," Inga said. She leaped off.

"Inga!" Cody yelled.

He dashed to the edge of the cliff. Mist obscured her as she fell. She didn't scream.

Oh no. What if she's hurt, what if—

The mist parted, and a pterodactyl burst up in front of him, flapping its wings. There was a blue band around its neck, and its eyes were unmistakably the glittering blue of Inga.

"You have to try this!" she called out. She did a flip in midair. "It's incredible."

Cody looked to Jayson, who was practically green.

"I hate heights," Jayson muttered.

Cody reached over and took Jayson's hand. Together, they jumped.

Light flared around him, beams of yellow that nearly blinded him. He closed his eyes, wincing against the light, and when he opened them again, he had turned into a pterodactyl.

He spread his arms wide on instinct and soared, Jayson roaring in excitement at his side. They flapped and flipped, momentarily lost in the exhilaration of flight. For one brief moment, it was easy to forget all his troubles and fears, easy to forget this had become a competition.

He had always wanted to fly. And now here he was!

Then someone screamed beside him, and the fun vanished.

30

Something rocketed past him, nearly knocking him from the sky.

It took him far too long to realize it was Inga.

"No!" he yelled out.

She plummeted toward the earth, but before he could race after her, claws scraped at his wings from behind. He yelped and spun in midair.

And faced another pterodactyl, this one with a red band painted around its neck and a fierce sparkle in its eyes.

Meg-A.

She opened her beak wide as if to bite him, but he tucked his wings in and dove down, racing after Inga.

Copper rings flashed past him as he dove, but he didn't bother going after them. Above him, he could hear Jayson yelling out for Meg-A to stop, but he quickly stopped being able to hear. The mist obscured him for a second, and then he passed through it, into a lush tropical jungle.

Inga lay sprawled across the top of a huge palm tree, her wings rumpled.

"Are you okay?" he asked, hovering beside her.

"Yeah," she replied. She shook her head. It was so strange hearing her voice come out of the pterodactyl's beak.

Oddly, hearing Meg-A's voice come from a monster wasn't such a stretch.

"That jerk just surprised me," Inga said.

"She's playing dirty," Cody said.

"I knew she would."

The fog above them parted, and the two of them readied for Meg-A's attack. But it was Jayson. He halted right beside Cody, flapping angrily.

"I can't believe—she shouldn't have—" he said, flustered.

"Where did she go?" Cody asked.

"Flew off," Jayson replied. "Ugh, when I see her again . . ."

"That doesn't matter," Inga interrupted. "We need to defeat her now. And we do that by winning this game."

She shook herself off and looked around. Dozens

of copper rings glittered in the air around them. For the moment, at least, it looked like the three of them were alone down here.

"Let's split up," Inga suggested. "Find as many rings as we can. And avoid Meg-A and her team at all costs."

Something roared in the undergrowth. Trees rustled in the distance.

"And avoid whatever *that* is," Jayson said. Cody nodded.

Above them, the score tracker jumped another twenty points. One of their opponents had found a silver, and the clock was ticking.

They darted off into the trees, each of them taking a different path. Wind whistled in Cody's ears as he ducked and twisted around branches and vines, snaring rings around his neck. The moment he touched them, they vanished in sprays of sparks. He felt a little thrill of victory each time. But Meg-A and her team were getting ahead.

He needed to go after the bigger scores. Fast.

But for that, he needed a better vantage point. Even if it did mean facing Meg-A's wrath.

He flapped higher, bursting through the cloud layer and up into the glittering sunlight.

What he saw made his stomach churn.

There were barely any more rings up in the air, at

least, not that he could see. And those that were still floating about were quickly being swept up by Meg-A and her team. They were easily four hundred points ahead of Cody, and gaining by the second.

He looked around wildly. They had to win. They just *had* to.

And there, above the gurgling volcano, he thought he caught a glimpse of something shining.

Something silver.

And something gold.

Monstrous birds circled around the volcano's mouth, but he didn't see Meg-A or anyone from his team heading that way. He had to risk it.

Keeping just above the clouds, he raced forward, catching a few stray bronze rings as he went. The clouds beside him billowed apart and Jayson rocketed by his side. It looked like there were rips in his wings, and he flapped awkwardly.

"What happened?" Cody asked, not slowing down.

"I was attacked. They weren't kidding about better rings being guarded. I was nearly eaten by a velociraptor! But I got a silver."

Cody feared that Inga might get in trouble, but he also knew she wouldn't want him coming after her. She'd want him trying to win.

"I think there are some rings at the top of the volcano," Cody said. "But it looks danger—"

The clouds before them burst apart, but it wasn't Inga coming to join them. The head of a ferocious T. rex reared up through the clouds, its reptilian eyes snaring onto them in a second. Each of its fangs was as big as Cody.

"Look out!" Cody yelped. He flapped to the side as the T. rex whipped its head toward him and nearly snared him in its jaws.

Jayson fluttered clumsily away, but the T. rex was fully focused on Cody.

The giant beast moved unnaturally fast for a creature that size. It snapped again at Cody, just barely missing one of Cody's wings. The monster's breath was hot and rancid and smelled like old dog and meat.

"Careful!" Jayson yelled.

Another T. rex appeared from below, its jaws reaching up and around Cody like a shark snapping up from the water.

As it closed its mouth, Cody knew he was about to be swallowed alive.

Darkness engulfed him. And for a moment, for one horrifying moment, he thought this might really be the end.

Then the T. rex roared, and the jaws opened wide, and Cody swooped free.

Only to find Inga, scratching at the T. rex's eyes while Jayson flapped about the other one.

Once Cody was out, Inga yelled, "Come on!" and sped toward the volcano.

Cody and Jayson were close behind.

"Rings," Cody panted. "Up there!"

"I know," Inga responded. "I saw them."

Cody glanced over his shoulder. The T. rexes were gone.

But someone else had spotted the rings.

Meg-A and her team rocketed toward the rings, and judging from how far ahead they were in the scoreboard, if they got there first, it was game over. There's no way Cody's team would be able to make up for lost points, not with all the time they'd already spent getting bronze rings and escaping the dinosaurs.

Cody flapped harder, and even Jayson managed to keep up his speed.

They raced up the volcano's side, heading toward its peak, where Meg-A and her friends were fast approaching, and where unknown monsters circled and spiraled. When they got closer, Cody realized they were a different type of flying dinosaur, these ones with feathered wings and vicious teeth in their sharp beaks, like carnivorous parrots.

The moment the monsters spotted Cody's and Meg-A's teams, they started to attack.

Their screeches filled the air as Cody and his teammates ducked and dove to avoid their piercing talons and jagged teeth. One monster managed to snag Cody's wing, and a sharp pain lanced through Cody's body.

But he kept flying, kept racing toward the hoops that glittered only a few dozen feet away.

One monster knocked Jayson to the ground. Inga rocketed on ahead, but Cody noticed that Jayson wasn't putting up much of a fight. His friend cried out, and Cody decided that if he had to choose Jayson or winning, he'd choose Jayson.

He circled back around and dove, crashing into the monster and sending it reeling. Once it righted itself, it raced back toward Cody. Cody managed to knock its head with one of his claws. The monster screeched in anger and took off.

"You didn't have to do that," Jayson gasped. "We aren't going to win now."

"You're worth more than winning a stupid contest," Cody said.

Above them, at the mouth of the volcano, the monsters screeched and dove. The score tracker jumped a hundred points for Cody's team.

And three hundred for Meg-A's.

It was all over. They'd lost.

The monsters froze.

Actually, *everything* froze. Cinders paused in midair, the breeze halted, the clouds stopped skidding around them. The game glitched.

Another voice filled the air.

"It is funny you should say that, Cody" came Mr. Gould's voice. There was no hologram this time, just his booming voice filling the simulation. "Because I think it is time that we change things up a bit. You see, we've grown bored of watching you play these silly games, safe and secure in the belief that they can't hurt you. Well, as I'm sure you're starting to discover, they *can* hurt you. They can hurt you very much. And we're just getting started."

Cody looked at Jayson. Even as a pterodactyl, Cody could tell that his friend was afraid.

"What is he talking about?" Cody asked.

"Starting now," Mr. Gould continued, "the rules have changed. The danger is now real. There are no extra lives, no kiddie modes. At the end of this week, those of you with the top three scores will be allowed to leave the park. The rest, I'm afraid, will perish. You are no longer playing to have fun. You are playing to survive." He chuckled. His words spilled like ice water in Cody's stomach.

"Oh, and one more thing. Should you think of just sitting around or trying to defy me, I would like to kindly remind you of the trackers you had injected. Should any of you step out of bounds, you will explode. I look forward to watching you all play.

"Now, resume."

As soon as he stopped speaking, the monsters above resumed their attack.

"He can't mean it," Jayson mumbled. "That was a joke, right? He can't mean it."

"I don't . . ." Cody managed. But he couldn't finish the sentence. Partly because he knew that Mr. Gould was telling the truth—the games really were

now life or death—and partly because the volcano
below his feet rumbled.

He looked to its peak.

To where massive plumes of smoke and ash billowed out.

The volcano was erupting.

Cody froze. Inga was still up there. He had to save
her, he had to—

A meteor of molten lava landed right beside him.
He yelled and flapped back, but still got splattered by
the embers. Holes burned through his wings. There
was no mistaking it this time—it *hurt*.

"We have to run!" Jayson yelled.

Cody nodded and flapped his injured wings. Jayson
struggled at his side. Fear filled Cody, but Jayson managed to get alight. Just as he did so, another shadow
flew overhead. It wasn't a comet. It was Inga.

"Hurry!" she yelled. "We have to reach the nest
before the game ends!"

"What nest?" Cody replied.

She didn't stop to answer, but Cody saw that there

was another large pillar of stone in the direction she was heading, hundreds of feet away. He was positive it hadn't been there before. But atop it was a huge nest of branches and bones.

He started toward it and realized they weren't the only ones racing there. Meg-A and her team were darting across the sky as well.

But there wasn't time to worry about them. Behind them, the volcano was erupting, spewing great globs of molten rock high into the air while impossible streams of lava spewed over the sides. Cody could hear the dinosaurs roaring and trampling away below as the lava filled the forest under them. Trees burst into flames and rivers hissed to steam. In no time at all, all he could see beneath them were endless fields of burbling lava.

And the lava was rising.

He dodged a lava meteor that rocketed toward him, just missing his wing. One after another, more molten meteors rained from the sky, making him and his friends dodge and weave to keep from being hit. They flapped harder and faster. Above them, the countdown timer proclaimed they only had twenty seconds to reach the nest. And with every second that passed, the lava below rose another foot. It was only a dozen or so feet below the edge of the nest.

If they didn't reach the nest soon, they'd never get the chance.

He flapped harder. Inga was nearly to the nest. Cody was right behind her, with Jayson at his side. Inga landed and yelled out in victory.

Just as one of Meg-A's friends slammed into Cody.

He reeled. His arm burst out in pain as his wing crumpled at his side. Meg-A cackled and dove toward him again, but he managed to twist out of the way just before she hit.

They were only a few feet above the lava. The heat was enough to make him sweat and tears burn in his eyes.

"What are you doing?" Jayson called out. "Didn't you hear Mr. Gould? The danger is real now!"

"I know!" The girl cackled gleefully. He thought he remembered Meg-A calling her Janette. She hovered above Cody, readying for the next attack. "Which just means one less in the competition!"

She dove again.

Cody flipped to the side just in time. Her claws grazed his side, and pain sliced through his body.

"Cody, come on!" Jayson yelled. He was just above the nest. Inga was inside, wrestling with Meg-A and her other teammate.

Although pain burned in his side, Cody knew the only way to end the game was to get into that nest with his friends. Before Janette or the lava ended him.

Janette dashed toward him again, this time from the side. And just as she neared, he rotated so that she flew right under him. In that moment, he pushed against her as hard as he could with his tiny pterodactyl legs and used that burst to catapult himself up.

The girl screamed, but he didn't look down. He had only a few seconds left. The lava was rising. Sparks and plumes of smoke filled the air. He could barely see. Could barely breathe.

With one last furious flap of his wings, he landed in the nest, beside Jayson and Inga, who had both managed to pin down Meg-A's team.

The moment he landed, sparks exploded around them.

Sparks, and then a blinding white light.

When he could see again, they were back in the Prehistoric Paradise. Inga and Jayson stood at his side, as did Meg-A and her teammate.

His wrist buzzed. He glanced down to see his watch declare that he and his team had lost, though they still earned a few points for playing.

"Where is she?" Meg-A asked. "Where did she go? Janette! Where are you?!"

Cody looked up. Looked around. His head was still in a daze from the game, from jolting back to reality.

It was only then that he realized that although her team had won, Janette was nowhere to be found.

33

"We know you did not mean to do it," Inga said. She patted his back, but it was far from comforting.

They sat in a café, this time in the Polar Adventure section of the park. Everything in here was crafted from ice and snow, from the robotic snowmen rolling about and delivering food to the icicle chandeliers above them. They were the only ones in the café, and the three mugs of hot chocolate and basket of cheesy fries between them were untouched.

Cody didn't think he'd be able to eat again. Not even if his life depended on it.

"I didn't want her to get hurt," Cody muttered for the millionth time. "I just thought I could get higher if I . . . I didn't want her to go into the lava. I didn't . . ."

"We know, Cody," Jayson said softly. "And no one blames you."

But that wasn't true. Everyone blamed him. At least, Meg-A did. She had nearly beaten him to a pulp, and probably would have if the other girl hadn't physically dragged her away as Meg-A yelled that she was going to call her lawyers when they got out of here and make sure that Cody paid.

Cody and Inga and Jayson had spent a full hour searching the plaza for any sign of Janette. But she was nowhere to be seen.

There hadn't been many other kids around, either. Those they saw looked shell-shocked. A few had asked if Cody and his friends had heard the horrible news. Others proclaimed that they, too, were missing friends. No one seemed to want to play any more games, now that they knew the danger was real. Cody among them.

"I wish I'd never heard of this place," Cody muttered.

"If you hadn't, you never would have met us," Jayson said.

"But Janette—"

"Look, Meg-A and her friends are all bullies," Inga interjected. "And although no one deserves to be hurt, we must believe that she wasn't . . . permanently harmed. Imagine the trouble the park would be in! She must be hidden somewhere."

"I don't think Mr. Gould cares about that anymore," Cody said. "He's already basically kidnapped all of us and put us in harm's way." As if to accentuate his point, the slash marks on his side from Janette's attack burned fiercely. He winced. But it just made a new fire burn in his chest. He looked up into one of the many cameras in the café—this one poorly camouflaged as a penguin sitting on a shelf—and yelled, "We aren't playing anymore, do you hear me?! We're done with your games."

The penguin didn't respond. Neither did Mr. Gould. Cody sighed.

"Why do you think they are doing this?" Inga asked.

Jayson shook his head. "Some sick joke," he replied. "He's got the whole world watching us, I'm sure."

"But why?"

"It doesn't matter," Cody said. "What matters is getting out."

"We can't," Inga said. "You heard what he said. I don't want to explode."

"Are you suggesting we play the games?" Jayson asked. "I don't want to get eaten by zombies or anything, either."

"No," Inga said. "But there has to be another way."

"What if there isn't?" Jayson asked. "What if he was telling the truth, and we either play, or die?"

"I don't want to play his games," Cody said.

"I don't either," Jayson admitted. He looked to the penguin camera. "But if we want to get out of here, we may not have a choice."

The park was subdued as they made their way back to the suites. It was late, and the sky was dark and studded with stars. No hint of a world outside of here. No promise that they'd ever make it out. Just a scoreboard, always ticking away on the horizon. There were a lot fewer names on it than there had been before.

"I don't know if I'll be able to sleep tonight," Inga said.

"Really? I'm exhausted," Jayson replied. They stood outside the hotels, bathed in lamplight. They were the only ones there.

"I am as well," she said. "But this just feels . . . wrong. It feels too calm."

Cody nodded. "Mr. Gould isn't going to be happy to see that no one is playing."

"Not now," Jayson said. "But people are going to start getting desperate when they realize they can't get out. They'll play then. When it's clear they have to win."

Just then, another kid appeared along the path. And for the first time since they'd arrived, Cody looked at the approaching boy with suspicion. Who knew what everyone else would do?

"We will figure this out in the morning," Inga said. "Just be careful. No games until we have sorted this out."

"Wouldn't dream of it," Jayson replied.

They parted awkwardly and made their way to their separate buildings.

When Cody looked over his shoulder and watched Inga disappear inside, a part of him feared he'd never see her again.

34

"Jayson?" Cody asked again, knocking on Jayson's door. It was already nine, and they were supposed to be meeting Inga outside. Jayson must be sleeping in. Celebrities. He knocked again, a little harder this time.

Truth be told, Cody still wanted to be in bed. He'd barely slept last night. He kept having horrible dreams: being chased by raptors, suffocating in space, falling off a roller coaster into lava. In all of them, Mr. Gould's voice had been a constant reminder that they were playing for real.

He'd woken up once in the middle of the night to a great rumble like thunder that shook his bed. But when he looked outside, nothing seemed amiss.

"Come on, Jayson, Inga's going to start worrying."

He pounded harder.

One of the doors beside him opened, and a boy Cody had never seen before poked his head out. He must have been one of the nobodies. Like Cody.

"What's wrong?" the boy asked.

"Nothing," Cody replied. "My friend's just sleeping in. Come on, Jayson, wake up."

"Maybe he already left?" the boy asked.

"No, we were supposed to meet here." He paused. "Hey, did you hear that loud explosion last night?"

The boy nodded. "I thought it was an earthquake."

Cody knocked again. This was getting ridiculous. He tried the handle, but it was locked.

"Did you hear the footsteps?" the boy asked.

Cody paused.

"What footsteps?"

"After the earthquake," the boy continued. "I was up for a long time. A few hours after it, I heard footsteps outside. And doors opening. I didn't think anything of it, but I think one of them was his door."

"That's strange," Cody said. "He wouldn't have left in the middle of the night."

"No. I heard strangers *come in,*" the boy replied. "I thought maybe he was having guests or something, and—"

Cody wasn't listening any longer. Fear burst through his chest as he kicked open the door. He didn't expect it to work, but the door slammed open.

Revealing an empty, unmade bed.

Jayson had been taken.

35

"They took him!" Cody yelled. "They took Jayson!"

"What?" Inga asked. "Who?"

"I don't know."

They stood outside the suites. A few other kids had gathered nearby. Jayson wasn't the only one who had been taken in the night.

It sounded like at least a dozen kids had been stolen in their sleep. And there had been no note, no hint as to why. Cody and the others stood around in shocked silence, or whispered conspiratorially. No one had any clue what to do, but it was clear that *going on rides* was the last thing on anyone's mind.

Just then, the sky flickered.

Mr. Gould's face appeared in the fluffy white clouds. He was smiling.

It was not a pleasant smile.

"So, you thought you could beat me at my own game, did you?" Mr. Gould asked. He laughed cruelly. "I could have put you in your places by detonating your trackers now. Just a few of you. Just to make a point. But explosions are only fun to watch for a few moments. And trust me when I say: The *whole world* is watching you now."

Hologram screens flickered in the air. News feeds. Websites. Livestreams.

All featuring ESCAPE.

Some showed a live feed of the park—including Cody and the others standing in the plaza *right now*—while the news ticker scrolled *Search continues for missing kids trapped in mastermind's theme park. No leads found.*

Hundreds of news stations from around the globe were watching.

Millions of people were tuning in.

And yet, apparently, no one knew where they were. Cody remembered the private drivers, the sleek cars. Even he had left home without a trace, and without the slightest idea where he was actually going. There had always been rumors about where the park was located, but never an exact address. Cody wondered if even those rumors had been fabricated ruses.

The screens flickered off, and it was just Mr. Gould's face once more.

"Don't let the news fool you, kids," he continued. "They don't want you to be rescued. No. They want a *show*. And you are going to give it to them. Or else."

"We aren't playing anymore!" Inga yelled to the clouds. "We're all done!"

"All of you?" Mr. Gould asked. "Because it seems to me that many of you are missing. And not just the ones who were injured in the games." He grinned wider as dread grew. "You think you've found a way to beat me, but I am—and always will be—ten steps ahead of you. Your friends have been hidden throughout the park. Hidden in the hardest games yet. Your watches will tell you which game to play. If you win, you can get your friends back. If you lose, well, you won't have to worry about your friends any longer. Oh, and should you even *consider* trying to thwart me again when your friends are rescued, let me assure you: This is just the beginning of the horrible things I can do to you.

"Put on a show for our eager fans. Remember: The top three scorers will be let free at the end of the week, and you will be stars. More famous than ever before. And that's what you all wanted, isn't it? To be famous? I'm giving you your chance.

"Now, go play. Or else."

The hologram flickered out.

A few of the kids around them started to sob. Others started to partner up or wander away through the park with renewed determination. One boy ran over and kicked a statue. The statue kicked back and sent him sprawling.

Cody's watch buzzed.

He looked to Inga. Her return gaze was resolute.

"Let's do this," she said. She reached out and took Cody's hand.

Together, they walked through the crowd and toward where their watches promised Jayson would be.

The horror park.

The horror park was hidden at the very edge of ESCAPE, past winding paths leading to much more inviting places, like Mount Olympus and Tropical Paradise. *Those* paths were filled with dense foliage and streams of morning light.

The farther they walked along the path taking them to the horror park, the less inviting it became.

The cobblestones at their feet slowly turned weathered and cracked, leaching to a bone white and gray. The trees around them grew gnarled and spindly, with ravens cawing in the branches and watching them with their beady camera eyes. Other shapes flitted through the trees, shapes Cody only ever caught from the corner of his eye. Shadows. Or pale green shimmers that looked an awful lot like ghosts. Even the sky lost its brilliance, fading from bright blue to a somber, cloud-filled gray, with no sun in sight.

There was no music here. Just the rustling of branches and caws of birds and crunch of bone-like gravel at their feet.

"Are you sure he is in here?" Inga asked. Her voice was barely a whisper.

Cody just nodded. He knew they were being watched, knew there were cameras everywhere—but this felt like a totally *different* sort of being watched. The sort that sent chills down your spine. The sort that didn't feel entirely human.

At any second, he expected something to scream in the distance.

At any second, he expected—

a skeleton burst from the trees beside them.

Cody screamed. Inga immediately kicked forward. The skeleton burst apart into a hundred bones. But they watched in horror as the bones spun and twitched back together, as the skeleton started to rebuild itself.

"Magnets," Cody breathed. "Has to be."

But what they were wasn't important, because more skeletons were clattering out around them. Skeletons with burning green eyes and sharp gnashing teeth and fingers whittled to claws. The skeletons shambled forward, surrounding them.

Forcing them farther into the horror park.

"Come on," Cody said.

They ran forward, dodging between skeletons that swiped at them, ducking as ravens swooped down from the branches and clawed at their heads. The specters Cody had seen before now swarmed around them, flickering in and out, wailing and moaning and reaching with transparent limbs.

"Is this part of the game?" Cody yelled out as he leaped over a jack-o'-lantern that rolled in front of him.

"You're the park expert!" Inga replied.

It struck him as strange, in that moment, because he didn't feel like an expert at all. He'd thought he'd known everything there was to know about the park before coming here. He didn't feel that way at all now.

If he did, he'd know how to get them out.

They raced forward. The ghosts and ghouls chasing them followed slowly, blocking off any hope of escape. Cody dared a quick glance at his watch.

Jayson was locked away in a ride called Tower of Tragedy. And it was easy to see which ride that was.

They reached the main plaza for the horror park. Tombstones toppled and towered around them, skeletons and ghouls clambering from the soil. There were graveyard mazes and haunted houses and pits of despair. And there, to their right, a huge tower reached into the stormy clouds.

It was tilted, teetering, with decaying gray shingles

and shattered windows emitting flickering purple light. Cody would have known that was the Tower of Tragedy even without the name spelled out in the rusted gate in front of it.

Cody began racing toward it, Inga close behind.

The plaza behind them crawled with undead monsters, and crows still swooped at their heads.

Still, Inga looked up at the tower and hesitated.

"I really do not want to go in there," she said.

"I don't either, but we have to rescue Jayson."

They raced up the broken path to the tower. Lightning crackled overhead and terrible laughter echoed from inside.

Then they yanked open the front door and began what Cody feared would be their last ride.

Silence descended the moment the door closed behind them, a silence so deep it felt like entering a crypt.

The only light in the foyer came from candles that somehow burned purple. Their flickering cold glow cast harsh shadows over the slate-gray walls; old Victorian paintings lined the walls, and cobwebs draped from the eaves like curtains. The floor beneath their feet was covered in tattered rugs, and with every step, small plumes of dust rose around them. A few pedestals lined the hall, topped with vases of dried and dead flowers. Cody couldn't look down the hall for too long—he swore the hall moved as he stared at it, flicking left and right like a serpent's tail.

"What do we do?" Inga asked. "What sort of ride is this?"

Cody glanced around. There was no cart to get in, no guide. Just the two of them in the entrance hall.

"I think maybe it's a maze," Cody said. "Or a fun house."

"Just do not tell me we have to split up."

"It *would* help us cover more ground," Cody said.

Inga just glared at him.

"Don't worry, I'm not abandoning you," he continued. "Together we can find him in no time. Besides, I need to keep you around in case any other monsters appear. That kick was spectacular."

Inga blushed as they started walking down the hall.

"Self-defense is important," she said.

Cody nodded. "You'll have to teach me. I'm a weakling."

She looked at him. "I do not think you are weak. You are smart. That is a strength."

"Yeah, but I'm not smart enough to figure out how to get out of here," he said.

"You will," she said. "I'm sure of it."

Cody wasn't certain how she could be so confident in him when she barely knew him, but it made him feel a little more confident in himself. There had to be a way out. *Had* to.

The hall split into three paths. One way was lit

with purple candles, the other blue, and the final green. They kept to the purple path, choosing without saying a word. When they weren't whispering to each other, the tower was quiet. Too quiet. He couldn't even hear their own footsteps.

So he kept talking, just to fill the void.

"Why did you come here?" he asked her. "I mean, you don't have to answer if you don't want to."

"No, it is okay," she replied. She looked at him levelly. "I came here because I hoped it would allow me to live like a normal kid. Everyone came here to escape from something. So many think they were escaping a boring life. I came here to escape *to* a boring life. Or a normal life. Where I wouldn't have cameras following me or people questioning my every move. I guess I was wrong."

"Is it really that bad?" Cody asked.

"Not always," she said. "I am very blessed. But it can also be quite isolating. It is hard to know if someone is your friend because they like you, or because they want to be famous. It makes it hard to trust."

Cody nodded. "I like you for who you are," he said. And he realized then that it was true. Sure, he'd idolized her and Jayson before meeting them, but now that he had met them, he felt like they were his friends. True friends. The type you'd invite over for pizza and movies and games. Like Patrick and Laura.

He wondered if all his friends would get along.

He wondered if he'd ever get the chance to introduce them.

"I wasn't telling the full truth before," he admitted. "I made it sound like I didn't care about coming here. The truth was, I was obsessed. I couldn't think of anything else."

"Was *your* life that bad?"

He thought about it. Sure, his parents always fought. But he had good friends back home, and he was doing well in school, and he had something he was truly passionate about: theme parks. He was pretty blessed as well. It was strange to realize that he actually sort of missed it all.

He was actually sort of excited to get back.

"No," he said. "But I thought it was. My parents are always fighting. But that wasn't all of it. I wanted to come here because, well, theme parks are like my biggest passion. I really want to build my own. I hoped if I came here, I'd be able to network or get inspired. Instead, I'm just trying to escape with my life."

Inga snorted. "So you're a theme park nerd?"

He looked at her. "Yeah," he admitted. "I guess so."

"That is cute," she replied. She smiled at him.

He reached over to take her hand . . .

And the floor beneath him dropped away, sending him plummeting.

38

"Cody!" Inga screamed out, right before the trapdoor shut and cut her off.

Cody quickly realized he wasn't falling straight down—he was sliding along, and within moments he'd landed in a pile of soft, squishy objects that he hoped were foam. There were no lights down here. He couldn't even see his own hands.

"Inga!" he called out. "Inga, I'm okay! Keep looking for Jayson! I'll come find you!"

He didn't know if she could hear him. But he didn't want to lose any time. Who knew what dangers lurked in the tower? Who knew what horrible tortures Jayson was being subjected to?

In darkness, Cody waded his way through the shifting bits of hopefully foam, trying to keep his arms up so he didn't touch anything. He also tried not to flinch when his raised hands grazed through spiderwebs. He moved slowly.

At least, until something *slithered* past his leg.

Then he moved a lot faster.

Eventually, he reached the edge of the pit that was holding him. A concrete wall at chest height, by the feel of it. He slowly, awkwardly lifted himself up out of the pit.

The moment he did, a light flickered on.

He was very grateful the lights had been out.

Because the moment he pulled his foot from the foam pit, he realized it hadn't been foam at all.

At least, not *all* foam.

The pit was filled with foam blocks. But coiled among them were spiders and snakes and skulls. Some of the bugs were moving, and more than one snake slithered away when the lights came on. And he had just waded through *that*.

But there was no time to freak out. He had to find Jayson. And Inga—though he had no doubt Inga could take care of herself.

He was in a tiny, stone-walled room. It looked like a dungeon, with one purple-flamed torch in the wall and a wooden door leading out. And the pit. But he tried not to look in there again.

Without a backward glance, he made his way through the door.

And the ride glitched.

The moment he stepped through, the torchlit walls pixelated.

Froze.

Flashed white.

Back.

White again.

And when the ride rebooted, he was no longer in a haunted tower.

He was on a pirate ship.

Rain and waves splashed him, soaking him in an instant, while pirates yelled and ran around him, hoisting sails and loading cannons while—a few dozen feet away—another ship with regal flags fired at them.

"Argh!" one of the pirates yelled, crashing into Cody.

"Sorry!" Cody replied, but the pirate was already running toward the side of the boat, where soldiers were climbing up and over. The entire deck was filled with shouts and screams, the thunder of cannons and muskets, the clash of steel. Lightning flashed in the sky alongside the cannon fire, casting everything in harsh white light.

Cody reeled as the ship tilted and someone else crashed into him.

"Sorry!" she yelled.

"Inga!" he yelped.

She caught herself and looked at him.

"Cody! What in the world is going on? One minute I was in a hall of haunted mirrors and the next—" She looked around at the chaos.

"I don't know," Cody replied. "I think the game is glitching."

He grabbed her and pulled her down just in time; a cannonball flew right overhead, crashing into the deck in a spray of splinters.

"Where's Jayson?" Inga asked. "Is he still in the tower?"

The deck swayed as more cannonballs hit home.

Cody heard someone yelling out above the din.

He looked up.

To the tallest mast.

To see Jayson, tied to the crow's nest at the very top.

39

"I hate heights," Cody moaned as he slowly made his way up the mast.

Inga was right behind him, urging him on.

Pirates and officers clashed below—none had noticed them climbing. Yet.

Jayson was squealing high above, his mouth gagged with even more rope. But even though he'd seen them, he hadn't stopped making noises.

A gut-wrenching groan rumbled in the air. The ship swayed dangerously. Cody's stomach squirmed in his chest and he clenched his eyes shut. They were so high up. The rungs were so slippery. He couldn't move.

"Cody," Inga said below him, her voice comforting

but desperate. "Cody, come on. You have to keep going."

"I can't," Cody moaned.

"You have to," Inga said. "We've been spotted."

Cody peeked through an eye and, sure enough, a pirate was clambering his way up the ladder below them. Twenty feet away.

Cody steeled himself. Reached up. Grabbed the next rung. And the next.

"That's it," Inga reassured him. "You're almost there. You're doing great. Just don't look down."

Jayson let out a particularly loud squeal.

The boat swayed to the other side.

Cody's hand slipped.

He looked down to see an enormous orange tentacle rising from the deep. And another. And another.

Great kraken tentacles rose up around them, some wrapping around the ships, others smashing the pirates and officers into the water. Cody saw the monstrous body of the kraken surface beside them; its gnashing beak looked razor sharp, and its plate-flat giant eyes narrowed in on him.

A tentacle rose toward him.

He hurried.

The tentacle swiped, but Cody managed to lean to the side, just enough that he missed it.

"Hurry!" Inga screamed. She kicked at the pirate

who was quickly overtaking them, his eyes murderous.

Cody hurried.

The tentacle swatted toward him again. Pixels briefly broke over the scene, everything blurring into blocks before snapping back to the horrible ocean scene. The tentacle kept coming.

But before it could hit, a golden arrow pierced it from above.

Cody looked up to see a chariot drawn by two winged horses fly across the sky.

What in the world? he thought.

The kraken screeched, and Cody pushed the question from his mind. Another golden arrow shot past him, narrowly missing his shoulder, and embedded itself in the captain's quarters.

Cody wondered if the archer was aiming for the kraken or for him.

He hurried up the last few rungs. Inga was right behind him.

As the ship lurched dangerously and began to sink, as the archer ahead wheeled back around for another shot, Cody pulled himself over the edge of the crow's nest and helped Inga up. They both ducked just in time to watch the archer fly past. Cody saw the figure, but he didn't know what he was seeing—the archer was golden, godlike, with a blinding breastplate and billowing hair. Was it some sort of Roman god?

Then the archer aimed an arrow at him.

Cody quickly loosened the ropes around Jayson. Jayson yelped in surprise and happiness and wrapped Inga in a hug.

That's it. They'd done it. They'd rescued him.

They'd won!

So why. . . ?

Cody looked over to see the charioteer archer nearing, the god's blue eyes snaring Cody to the spot.

They had won, so why was the ride not ending?

The archer raced toward them.

The kraken raised its tentacle.

The pirate pulled himself up over the crow's nest.

They were trapped.

"Jump!" Cody yelled.

He grabbed Jayson's hand, who latched onto Inga. The three of them leaped over the railing and plummeted toward the churning ocean below.

They hit.

Breath burst from Cody's lungs as cold crashed into him.

He spluttered. Lost hold of Jayson's hand.

As lightning flickered above, Cody saw huge shapes swimming below them. Not just the kraken.

Sharks. Hundreds of sharks circling. Rising.

Racing toward him.

Cody screamed as a shark neared, its jaws open and teeth ready to rip him apart.

The water glitched.

Pixelated.

Flashed white.

Static hissed in his ears, and the next thing he knew he was splashing around in a pool.

No, not a pool. A fountain.

A fountain in the Roman Festival part of the park. A statue with winged shoes sprayed water into the shallow pool, and around them, great columns supported signs for Minotaur Maze and Prosperina's Escape.

Jayson and Inga floundered beside him.

It took them all a few moments to realize that they were back. They were off the ride, out of the game. Back in the main park. And for the moment, they were completely alone.

"What in the *world* just happened?" Jayson yelled. He rushed over and wrapped Cody in a tight hug. "Also thank you thank you thank you! But what was that?"

Cody hugged Jayson back. Then Jayson splashed over to Inga and hugged her, too.

"I don't know," Cody admitted. "The park is glitching out somehow."

"So I gathered," Jayson said. "But what happened?

I was in bed and then someone put a bag over my head and smuggled me away. The next thing I knew I was locked in a coffin beside what I'm pretty sure was a vampire."

"The game has changed," Inga said. "Mr. Gould is forcing us to follow his command. He captured a bunch of kids and hid them throughout the park so we would play."

"I knew I didn't like him from the very beginning," Jayson muttered.

The three of them stepped out of the fountain and looked around. The empty ride entrances beckoned.

"So what do we do?" Jayson asked. "Can we fight him? Build a ladder and scale the walls?"

Cody looked up.

The sky was washed in a beautiful pink sunset. Then it pixelated. Became a cosmic starscape. Before glitching again to noon.

"It's concrete," he said. "We're underground. I thought I noticed it the first day. Everything is a hologram. Even if we built a ladder, there's nowhere to go. And . . ."

"And?" Jayson asked.

"And if we try to leave," Inga finished, "Mr. Gould will detonate our trackers."

Jayson swallowed.

"So . . . what are we going to do?"

Cody looked over to one of the statues. He was certain there was a camera. Certain it was watching him. His thoughts raced. They hadn't *stopped* racing since Inga complimented him about knowing everything about the park.

He had an idea.

"We're going to play," Cody said, straight toward the statue. "And we're going to win."

41

"This doesn't feel right," Inga said as they made their way past the entrance of Minotaur's Maze.

Jayson looked up to the scoreboard in the sky. "Because there's no way we're going to win? We're all three of us *way* behind."

Cody glanced up. It was true—even though they'd each gotten a few hundred points for rescuing Jayson, they were light-years away from being in the top three.

"No," Inga said. "This is what Mr. Gould wants. He wants us to play the games and battle. He wants to prove that we are greedy and selfish and self-centered. We won't win, even if we make the top three, because that means we are abandoning everyone else. We are leaving them to die."

"Do you have a better idea?" Cody asked. He wheeled around to look at her. His voice shook. He tried to keep it firm. "Or do you want to just give up now?"

Inga looked hurt.

"Of course I do not want to give up. But that does not mean I feel right letting everyone else perish."

"It's not about them," Cody said. "I came here to win. And that's what I'm going to do. I don't care about everyone else."

He said it loud, boldly. Inga's concern grew.

"This does not sound like you at all," she said.

They had just reached the front of the line. Two stone minotaur statues flanked either side of the dungeon door. Their horns were steel, their axes sharp, and their eyes were unmistakably cameras.

"You don't know anything about me," Cody said.

"Yes, we do," Jayson chipped in. "We can't just play the games and leave everyone behind. It's . . . cruel."

"What would you know about cruel?" Cody asked. "You've been given everything in life. You have it all! This isn't just about getting out, don't you see? Don't you remember what Mr. Gould said? Whoever leaves here will get to be *famous*."

"Fame isn't everything," Inga insisted.

"That's easy to say when you already have it,"

Cody replied. "You don't know what it's like to be normal. To be completely unknown. It's the worst! This is my chance to make it big. I'm not going to let it go just because you're worried about a bunch of kids you've already admitted you hate."

"We don't hate them," Inga said. "Not at all."

"You said you don't like them. That you're not certain if they're even your real friends or not."

Inga's mouth opened. She looked like she'd been slapped. Cody's heart broke, but he continued on.

"Look, I don't care if you join me. But you said it yourself—I know everything there is to know about the park." He tried to give them a meaningful look. "So if you want to win, you'll follow me. If not, go back and hang out with the rest of the losers. I really don't care."

Jayson and Inga looked at each other. The relief Jayson had before for being rescued was gone, replaced with confusion and sadness. Inga looked at Cody like she didn't know him anymore.

But you do, he wanted to say. *You do.*

Jayson nodded to Inga. She shrugged.

"We will follow you," she said. "But that does not mean I like it."

"Yeah," Jayson said. "I mean, you saved my life. I owe you. And you're our friend. I think."

"I am," Cody said. "Trust me, you want to be on my team. Now, let's go beat this game."

He looked up at the minotaur statues. He knew they were looking back.

He strode forward, through the dungeon door, and down the stone steps into the dark.

42

At the bottom of the cold stone steps was another wooden door, and before it, a brown owl perched on the pedestal. At its feet were three wands.

The moment they neared, the owl's head twisted around, blinking to reveal two large golden eyes.

"Beware, mortals," the owl hooted. "Beyond this gate is the minotaur's maze. Inside, you will have only your wits and a bit of magic to guide you. At the heart of the maze is the minotaur's treasure. If you don't find it before the time is up, you will be trapped in his lair forever."

"Sounds a lot like the Anubis ride," Jayson muttered.

Cody picked up one of the wands. It was warm and buzzed like static in his hands.

"I will teach you three spells," the owl said as Inga and Jayson each grabbed their wands. "The first is for light. Envision a glow, and wave your wand before you, like this." It crossed a wing in front of it. Cody felt a little stupid, but he visualized a glowing light and slashed his wand. A moment later, a small orb of white appeared above him. Inga and Jayson did the same.

The owl taught them two more spells—one to create a gust of wind, and the other to create a shield—but even though Cody had once thought doing magic would be the coolest thing here, he felt numb.

He couldn't shake the disappointment he'd seen in Inga's eyes. The regret in Jayson's.

This should have been fun, but it was the furthest thing from it.

When they'd learned their spells, the door opened, and the three of them crept warily inside. The moment they passed the threshold, the door slammed and locked behind them, and their watches buzzed with a countdown.

Stone tunnels greeted them. Five tunnels, snaking off up and down, left and right and forward. There was no telling which way to go. But Cody had an idea.

Especially because, a moment later, a roar from one of the hallways rumbled their bones.

The minotaur was approaching.

"Let's go!" Cody urged. He raced off, down the stairs leading even deeper into the maze.

To their credit, neither Inga nor Jayson asked

where they were going or how he knew the way or who put him in charge. It was clear neither of them really wanted to be here. They were just going along with it. Because they trusted him.

Or had.

They were halfway down the hall when it split again. Cody took the left path without hesitating, though all the paths looked the same down here: Everything was the same stone walls, the same gravelly floor, the same evenly spaced torches on the wall. After a few more turns, it was impossible to tell which way they'd come from, but Cody kept guiding them forward.

Jayson walked quickly at Cody's side. "What do you think they gave us the wands for?" he asked. He flicked his wand, sending a small gust of air in front of them. A few torches guttered, but nothing else happened. "It's not like we need them."

"Maybe there are traps later on," Inga suggested. "Or puzzles."

They rounded the corner, and standing in the center of the hall were two obstacles Cody had *not* expected.

Meg-A and her friend.

"Or maybe," Meg-A said, "they're for fighting *us*."

She raised her wand, and when she brought it slashing down, a billow of flame erupted in front of her, lashing straight toward Cody.

Cody froze in shock, but Inga was faster. She jumped in front of him and waved her wand. A shield glimmered in the air in front of them, and the flames bounced harmlessly off. But Meg-A's friend ran forward, tackling Inga to the ground and dissolving the magical shield.

"Get off her!" Cody yelled. He leaped into action. A quick slash of his wand and a gust of air knocked the girl off Inga. She flew to the side but quickly got back on her feet.

Meg-A raised her wand and sent another burst of fire at them. This time, it was Jayson's shield that blocked it. But it was clear that the three of them were no match for Meg-A and her friend. Not when Meg-A had learned how to attack.

"Run!" Cody yelled. "This way!"

He pulled Inga to standing and yanked her back down the hall they had come from, Jayson keeping pace behind. He ran backward, casting shield after shield as Meg-A laughed maniacally and kept up an onslaught of flames.

"How did she learn offensive spells?" Inga asked.

"I don't know, but we have to—"

Whatever they had to do was knocked from his lips when they rounded the next corner. Because there, towering in front of them, was the minotaur, its ax held high.

"Look out!" Inga yelped. She cast a quick shield as the minotaur struck. His ax bounced off, but Cody doubted it would hold. He cast another gust of wind, trying to push the minotaur to the side.

But the beast didn't budge.

Jayson slammed into Cody's back.

"Why aren't we running?" he asked. Then he looked over his shoulder at the minotaur and yelped.

Cody looked around frantically. This wasn't how this was supposed to go. This wasn't—

The minotaur bellowed. Raised its ax for what would surely be a killing blow.

The game glitched.

The minotaur exploded into pixels.

And when the game rebooted, they were no longer

in the maze. They were on a raft, rocketing down a surging river.

"What, no!" Cody yelled.

He looked around frantically. The maze and the minotaur and Meg-A were nowhere to be seen. Instead, they were surrounded by thick leafy foliage and rocky beaches. The sky above was dazzling blue, and the river coursed rapidly forward. The three of them were on a bamboo raft, with only a single pole to guide them.

They still had their wands.

Jayson collapsed to the raft with a sigh.

"What are you so upset about?" he asked. "The minotaur's gone. We escaped."

"We need to go back," Cody said.

"What? Why?" Inga asked, raising her eyebrow.

"Because we have to finish the game! It's the only way to get points."

Jayson looked at him like he was losing it. "You want to go *back* there? Dude, you—"

CRASH!

The raft spun out of control as it hit a large boulder. If not for Inga's quick reflexes, Cody would have been thrown clear into the raging waters. And when he looked, he realized the water wasn't empty— crocodiles swam through the current as though it were nothing, their eyes watching the trio hungrily.

Jayson clutched wildly at the ropes as the raft thrashed through the river.

A roar filled Cody's ears.

He looked ahead to see a wall of mist.

A waterfall. They were about to go over a waterfall.

"Quick!" he yelled. "Grab the pole!" He dropped his wand and grabbed the steering pole.

Another roar bellowed. Cody thought it was the waterfall getting closer, but when he looked again it wasn't just a wall of mist.

The minotaur had appeared downstream. And it was sloshing slowly toward them, its ax raised and ready.

Inga stepped to the front of the raft. She waved her wand. Nothing happened.

"It only works in that one game!" Cody yelled.

"I realize that!" she yelled back.

She looked around for a weapon, any weapon, but the game glitched again.

Momentum carried them forward, sent them sprawling.

They landed on dry land. But it was not dry land Cody wanted to be in.

They had landed in a graveyard.

They scrambled to their feet.

"Okay," Inga said. "What. Is. Happening?"

"How are we supposed to win a game if it keeps glitching?" Jayson yelled to the dreary sky. "Your park bites!"

Lightning answered him.

As did the groans of the undead as they crawled out of their graves.

Jayson latched onto Cody as dozens of zombies pulled themselves from the ground. Their skin was gray and green and hanging off in strips. Their eyes were missing or dangling from empty sockets. And their smell . . . Cody knew they were just simulations, but they *really* smelled like rotting meat.

"I told you I didn't want to have my brain eaten by zombies!" Jayson yelped.

"No one's brains are getting eaten," Cody said.

But the zombies crowded around them in a semi-circle. There was only one way to go, and that was toward a dilapidated house that Cody was *sure* was going to be haunted.

The zombies shambled forward. Jayson peered out from behind Cody and waved his wand. "Back, zombies! Back!"

Against all odds, a gust of wind billowed from Jayson's wand.

Jayson let out a squeal of delight. Cody kicked himself for tossing his wand.

"Take that!" Jayson yelled, waving his wand again. Another breeze billowed out, knocking a nearby zombie to the ground.

"That's fun and all, but we really must find the exit," Inga said. Because while Jayson was playing wizard, dozens more zombies had risen from the grave. Hundreds surrounded them, and Cody had no doubt that soon there would be hundreds more.

"Toward the house!" he yelled.

They began to jog toward the haunted house, but they didn't make it three steps before a scream made them freeze.

Meg-A.

Cody squinted. He could just see Meg-A and her friend a few hundred yards off. They were surrounded by zombies. And it was clear neither of them had their wands, or any other weapon.

Cody groaned. For all his talk about getting to the top, he couldn't just leave them there to get eaten. Even if the two bullies deserved it.

"We have to save them!" he yelled.

"Are you crazy?" Jayson asked. The zombies were closing in. He cast another gale, and the zombie stumbled back. "We'll never make it."

"We cannot leave her," Inga agreed.

Jayson moaned, but there wasn't time to argue. "Fine!"

He stepped in front of Cody and started swinging his wand wildly. Wave after wave of wind billowed around him, forcing the zombies back and carving out a writhing pathway for them to follow. With Jayson in the lead, they made their way through the zombie horde. Gnarled hands reached out to grab at them, only to be pushed back by a last-minute magical blast. Rotted teeth gnashed hungrily for Cody's tender flesh, only to be blocked by a quick shield. The zombies closed in around them, with only the quick wand-work of Jayson keeping the zombies at bay.

Cody couldn't even see Meg-A anymore. But her screams guided them on.

Finally, Jayson cleared away the last zombies, and the trio broke through into the cleared graveyard. Cleared, except for the dozen or so zombies that surrounded Meg-A and her friend, who were pinned to the side of a mausoleum.

"Hey, boneheads!" Jayson yelled.

One of the zombies turned, only to be blasted away by a gust from Jayson's wand.

Jayson cleared the zombies, and Inga and Cody raced forward.

"I can't believe you saved us," Meg-A said. "I didn't think—I was so scared."

"Don't worry about it," Cody replied. "Come on, we have to get back to the maze. I mean, that manor. I think it's the exit."

They hobbled forward, the zombies shambling behind them.

Cody's mind raced. They had to get out of here. They had to—

A roar behind them made his blood freeze.

The minotaur was back.

It unfurled itself from inside the mausoleum, towering above them all. Meg-A screamed. Jayson tried another spell, but the wind billowed it off.

"Run!" Cody yelled.

They booked it. Toward the manor, toward another unknown horror, while the minotaur raced after them and the zombies shambled behind. Cody looked back once to see the minotaur galloping through a crowd of zombies—it carved a path through them with its broadax as easily as if they were grass. Lightning flashed in the sky.

The minotaur was gaining on them.

They'd never make it.

They'd never—

Lightning flashed again, only this time it wasn't lightning. The world went white with static. A fierce electric buzz. And when they could see again, they were back in the underground maze. Still running.

The minotaur was behind them. As were a dozen shambling zombies.

Cody yelled in frustration but continued to run, the breath burning in his lungs as the minotaur chased them down in its own domain.

"We aren't going to get anywhere like this!" Inga panted at his side.

Cody ducked down a side passageway. This one wasn't like the others. Rather than torches, a fire in a big brazier burned at the end of this hall. Hope sparked in his chest.

"This way!" he yelled.

They ran down the corridor and toward the fire, pausing for a second when they got to the circular chamber. A cauldron of flames burned in the middle. Five more tunnels stretched on all sides.

"We're doomed!" Jayson yelled.

But hope was finally blossoming in Cody's chest.

"We have to split up," he said. "You four go that way." He pointed to the tunnel that spiraled down. "The exit is through there. Keep going straight, then it's the second tunnel to your right."

"Why aren't you coming with?" Inga asked.

"If the minotaur follows you, you'll never make it," Cody replied.

"I don't understand," Inga whispered. "How do you know this—"

"Just go!" Cody said. The minotaur bellowed farther down the hall. It had found them. It was closing in. And the low moan of the zombies said they weren't far behind.

Jayson handed Cody his wand. "Take this," Jayson said. "You'll need it."

Cody thanked him and looked at them. "Go!" he yelled. "I'll draw it away."

Tears filled Inga's eyes, but she didn't protest. She nodded. Squeezed his shoulder. Then she and Jayson and Meg-A and her friend turned and ran down the hallway he'd pointed out.

Cody steeled his nerves. Turned toward the hallway the minotaur was coming down.

He waved the wand and sent up a ball of light. Then he cast a billow of wind, knocking over a nearby statue.

"Hey! Over here! Come get me!" he yelled as his friends disappeared to safety.

The minotaur roared. And when Cody saw its red eyes in the dark tunnel, he took off.

It's time to end this, he thought. One way or another, he would.

Cody raced through the tunnel. It spiraled upward, and soon he was panting, gasping for stagnant air—he'd never run so much in his entire life—but there was no time to pause or catch his breath. The minotaur was right behind him, its ax scraping along the stone walls, and the zombies were running to keep pace.

His ruse had worked. But if he didn't keep up the pace, it would work *too* well.

Eventually, the tunnel evened out again. This tunnel, however, was lined with torches that burned a brilliant white.

This is it.

He ran harder.

Halfway down the wall he spotted it. A torch that burned just a little less white, a little more orange. He slowed down. Blood pounded in his ears but victory rang in his chest.

He slid his hands along the stone wall, looking for what he'd seen before.

Looking for what he'd seen in a long-since-deleted video.

Ages ago, when ESCAPE had started releasing its promotional videos, he'd watched a clip of a kid running down this very hallway. Running from the very minotaur that chased after him.

The clip had only been up for a few minutes—not even three minutes, tops—before it was taken down by the admin. But he'd seen it.

And it had been taken down because, in the clip, you could see the outline of a slightly open door in the wall, otherwise hidden in the stonework.

A door leading into a pristine white hallway that Cody knew must be an exit.

Cody's fingers traced the stones. He hoped against hope that they hadn't taken the door away. He was *sure* this was the right spot. It had to be.

A stone clicked beneath his fingers. On the other side of the wall, he heard alarms go off.

He'd found it!

A roar filled the tunnel.

The minotaur had found *him*.

46

The minotaur swung.

Cody ducked just in time to miss the ax that slashed at his head. The ax crashed into the door, knocking it shut.

Farther on, Cody saw the zombies shuffling quickly; if he didn't get out of here soon, he'd never get the chance.

The minotaur bellowed and raised its ax again. Cody tried to cast a gust of wind at it, but the breeze didn't do a thing—the minotaur was too large, or the spell was too weak. As the ax fell, he cast a shield spell and winced as the heavy blade struck, the ax pausing in midair. His whole body vibrated from the shock as he struggled to keep the shield up.

A zombie swiped at him from the side.

Cody leaped out of the way. The shield dissipated, and the ax slammed into the ground right where Cody had just been.

The zombies continued moving forward, edging Cody away from the door. Away from his only means of escape.

He cast a gust of wind at them, but all it did was push them back slightly. They were so jammed together, it wasn't doing much at all.

The minotaur swung again, and Cody had to roll out of the way to avoid being crushed. Every step away from the door made panic amp up in his veins. He couldn't let them push him too far. This was his only shot.

As the minotaur raised its ax again, Cody remembered how the monster had plowed through the zombies earlier without pausing. A dangerous idea brewed in his mind.

He cast a shield around him, hoping it would hold, and as the minotaur swung, he crouched and raced forward, hiding in the crowd of zombies.

Zombies clawed at him as he ran through, their hands grazing across the shield. When he was in the middle of them, he huddled on the ground with his wand raised, trying to maintain the shield.

The ax sliced through the air just above his head. It cut through the zombies—where the ax hit, the zombies vanished in a cloud of pixels and ash. Within seconds, the zombies surrounding the door were gone. Only a handful of them remained, but they were too far off to be a threat.

Cody didn't wait around.

While the minotaur readied its ax, Cody ran to the secret door and yanked it open.

Blinding white light greeted him. The hallway was pristine, with white tile floors and walls and silver pipes stretching along the white ceiling.

He leaped through the door. Into the frigid hallway.

He watched as the minotaur madly swung its ax. But it was part of the simulation. It couldn't get through.

Cody was safe.

He gasped in relief and flopped back on the cold tile floor.

He'd made it.

He was out.

"What do you think you're doing here?" Mr. Gould asked.

Cody wasn't alone.

Mr. Gould yanked Cody up to standing.

For being a mad scientist, he was actually pretty strong.

"Get off of me," Cody growled. He shoved at Mr. Gould, who dropped him to the tiles. Cody took a few steps back.

"You aren't supposed to be out of the game," Mr. Gould said. He looked just as he had before, in the same fancy suit, with the same messy hair. But something had changed in his eyes. He no longer looked warm and inviting.

He looked like a wild animal.

He pointed back to the door. "How did you even know that existed?"

"I saw it in one of the videos you took down. I'm

the park's biggest fan," Cody replied. "At least, I was until I learned what you were doing."

Mr. Gould smiled. "Have me all figured out, do you? So why, Cody—yes, I know your name, just as I know everything there is to know about you—why do you think I have gone to all this trouble?"

"Because you're jealous," Cody said. "Jealous of their fame, jealous of their—"

"Jealous?!" Mr. Gould cackled. "You really think I'm jealous of *them*? Or you? Please. This has nothing to do with jealousy. This has to do with setting things right."

"You're hurting kids. How could that set anything right?"

"Because the world needs to be taught a lesson," Mr. Gould said. His jaw muscles twitched, and anger burned in his eyes. "I brought in the most famous kids on the planet. Why? Not because I was jealous, no. But because they spend their entire lives in front of the camera; you all live and die in front of your phones, all in the name of—what? Fame? *Connection?* Please. Look what happened in there! The moment it became a competition, the moment you knew it was *real*, you were at each other's throats. Because you knew it would make you even more famous. You would all do anything to get to the top. You're all *monsters.*"

"Not everyone in there is famous," Cody began, but Mr. Gould cut him off.

"As if that makes you any better than them? I told you, Cody—I know everything about you. I know that you've spent the last three months dreaming of a chance to come here. You tell yourself it's because you want to build a park for others to enjoy. But in truth? It's because you want to feel important. Popular. Famous. You want to be among the elite just like everyone else in the park. But you, you're even worse than the celebrities. They live their lives for other people. But you, Cody, you've given up your childhood following the lives of people you never even *knew* before coming here. How pathetic is that?"

Mr. Gould's words were a punch to the gut. He tried to stay angry, but it was hard when it felt like the man was speaking the truth.

"You're never getting away with this," Cody said.

"I already have," Mr. Gould said. "You've already proven my point."

"No. There are good kids in there. My friends—"

Mr. Gould howled with laughter. "Friends? You? Do you really think those two celebrities will even think of you when the game is over? You're a friend of convenience, Cody. Nothing more."

"That's not true," Cody whispered, even as he thought, *It isn't, is it?*

"You know it is. Deep down, you know you aren't worth anything." Mr. Gould crept closer. Behind him, the open door of the park beckoned. Cody could just make out the zombies and minotaur still crowded around beyond.

But he wasn't focused on them.

Memories surged in Cody's head. His parents fighting. His dad ripping down all his posters, all his dreams. The nights he'd spent staring out the window, wondering if his life would ever feel important. Worth something.

Except . . .

Other memories swirled. Fresher memories. Inga's laugh. Jayson's kindness. Cody *knew* they weren't friends of convenience. They liked him for who he was. And he liked them for who they were. It had nothing to do with fame. Nothing to do with celebrity. They were his friends. Just like Laura and Patrick back home were his friends.

To them, he was something.

And that was enough.

"No," Cody said. He glared at Mr. Gould.

"No?"

"No. It's over. I'm getting my friends out. We're done playing."

"I'm afraid it isn't that simple," Mr. Gould said. He reached into his pocket and pulled out a remote.

"All I have to do is push this one button, and you will explode. Now, get back in the park and play. Play to win. And maybe you'll get your wish."

"You're lying," Cody said. "If those trackers were set to explode, you'd have made a fail-safe. Made it so anyone who stepped out of the park would blow up the moment they were out of bounds. You would have made an example. It's a fabrication, just like everything in your park."

Mr. Gould didn't look angry. Instead, he grinned.

"Figured that out yourself, did you? I guess you're smarter than I thought. But that won't help you."

He stepped forward, arm outstretched.

Cody swiped his wand, imagining the gust spell.

Nothing happened.

Mr. Gould paused and laughed again.

"Maybe you aren't so smart as I thought. Stupid child. I'm not wearing a suit. That doesn't work on me. As you said, *it's all a fabrication.*"

"I know," Cody said. He grinned. "I just needed you to hesitate."

With that, he ran forward and kicked Mr. Gould in the chest, just like he'd seen Inga do in the games.

Mr. Gould staggered backward.

Toward the door.

Toward the zombies.

Toward the minotaur.

The moment he tripped back over the threshold, the zombies grabbed him, pulled him back. Mr. Gould started to yell out for help.

"So much for fabrications," Cody said.

He shut the door behind Mr. Gould, trapping him in his own creation.

48

Cody raced down the white hallway, everything a blur.

He partly guided himself by his gut, and partly from clips he'd seen on ESCAPE's feed. He'd seen these halls before in their exclusive behind-the-scenes videos.

Surprisingly, he didn't run into anyone else.

Not a single soul. Nor were there any cameras here, or robotic guards.

Apparently, Mr. Gould put all his efforts on keeping kids inside the theme park. He hadn't given a thought to what would happen if one of them got out.

Finally, he made his way to the control room. Glass windows overlooked the theme park. From here, Cody could see plumes of smoke and tendrils of fire, just as he could see kids running around.

He even thought he could see Inga and Jayson huddled in the main square below.

Cody looked around. The room was filled with computers and wires, buttons and screens. But he remembered a video, one of the first videos posted. Of Mr. Gould standing in this very room, standing before *that* very computer, beaming at the camera and saying that this was where the magic was created.

Cody stepped forward. Looked to the very expensive-looking computer.

Mr. Gould thought he and the others had spent their lives ignoring the real world. He was wrong. Cody had been paying attention. He'd been paying attention from the very beginning.

Cody typed in the password he'd seen Mr. Gould key in during that video. A random series of numbers and letters that he'd memorized. Just because. Just in case.

The park's command screen pulled up. And at the very top was a red button.

DEACTIVATE

Cody clicked it.

In the theme park, the holograph sky flickered. Went out. Revealed a ceiling of oppressive concrete. He couldn't hear anything, but he could imagine a collective whir as the rides shut down. As the simulations ended.

He clicked the button to open the door, and then he picked up the microphone beside the computer.

A camera blinked on, and his image was projected onto the ceiling inside the park.

Cody grinned. *He* was the one on-screen now.

"It's over," he said to the trapped kids. "Everybody out. It's time to make our escape."

EPILOGUE

"You're sure you can't come with?" Inga asked.

They were in the hotel lobby—him and Inga and Jayson. Even Meg-A was there.

Two days had passed since they had managed to escape from ESCAPE. Once they were out of the park, most of the kids had left, never wanting to look back. After they'd all been questioned by the authorities, that was. But Cody and his friends—even Meg-A, whose name was actually Meredith—had decided to stay together a bit longer. Once he'd borrowed Jayson's phone to call home, he'd had to beg his parents, but they relented when they knew he was safe and with friends. They'd been watching him on the news. Everyone had. And one of the last things his dad said before hanging up was *I'm proud of you.*

Cody would remember that forever.

"I gotta go home," Cody said. "But next time! I swear!"

"I'm holding you to that," Jayson said. He poked Cody's duffel bag with a toe. "Though we're getting you designer bags before then. There's no way we're flying a private jet to Iceland with *that*."

Cody laughed, and Jayson grinned. Once, he might have felt bad because of the joke. But he knew that Jayson and Inga saw him as an equal.

Most importantly, he *knew* he was.

"Well, we will miss you," Inga said. "Promise to keep in touch."

"Of course," he replied. "Wouldn't miss it for the world."

He paused.

"Actually, I wanted to apologize," he said, looking at them all. "For what I said earlier. I hope you know I didn't mean any of it. I had to convince everyone watching that I was just focused on winning the games—if they knew I was trying to get out, they would have tried to stop me."

"We figured," Jayson said. "You aren't a bad guy. Though you *are* a good actor. Seriously, you should consider a career change. If you ever need pointers, I know a guy—"

Meg-A laughed. "Please. Cody would be better off

with *my* agent. We have much stronger connections."

Jayson looked like he was about to argue, but Cody stopped them both.

"I think I'm good," he said. "Acting isn't for me. I still feel pretty horrible for even pretending to be mean to you."

"I feel bad, too," Meg-A said. "I lost myself in there. But, well . . . after Janette went missing, I decided to take matters into my own hands. I went into one of the cafés in the middle of the night and maybe kind of blew it up."

"That was you?" Jayson asked incredulously. Admiration gleamed in his eyes.

"Yeah," Meg-A replied. "I think that might be why the games started glitching."

"We owe you, then," Cody said. "We wouldn't have gotten out otherwise."

"Which," Inga said, "has anyone heard—did they find Mr. Gould?"

They all looked at one another in silence. They shook their heads.

After the park was deactivated, *all* the missing kids had been recovered. A few had been injured, but they were all okay. Just locked away in holding cells.

Mr. Gould, however, had never been found.

"Let's just hope the zombies ate him," Jayson said. "Serves him right."

"Yeah," Cody said. "We don't need any more evil masterminds running loose in the world."

"Not when there's already you," Jayson replied with a wink.

The hotel door opened, and Cody's dad appeared. He gave Cody a little wave.

"Okay, I gotta go," Cody said. He gave Jayson and Inga and Meg-A a hug. "I'll miss you."

"Don't say that," Inga replied. "We aren't leaving you." She smiled warmly.

He knew she was telling the truth.

He grabbed his bags and walked toward his dad, who quickly swept him up in a hug and offered to carry his luggage.

Cody looked back just once while leaving the hotel.

He wasn't leaving his dream life behind.

He was going to be living it.

ACKNOWLEDGMENTS

I've always loved theme parks.

Actually, let me clarify: I've always loved the *ideas* behind theme parks. Like Cody, I'm fascinated by what goes on behind the scenes on all the interactive rides. I could spend hours watching documentaries on how rides are made, and once thought that my future career was in special effects and ride creation. Turns out, I ended up following a different interest, so I'm grateful to be given a chance to write about one of my many hobbies!

To that end, my biggest thanks goes to David Levithan, Jana Haussmann, and the entire Scholastic and Fairs teams for making this book a reality. I had such a blast writing it, and wouldn't have been able to do it without your enthusiastic support and editorial insight. After all these years of writing creepy tales, it was so much fun to create something that was pure adrenaline and technical wizardry. Here's to making many more wild fantasies come true!

As always, my eternal gratitude goes to my parents and family. I was so, so lucky to have parents who allowed me to explore my hobbies. Their support helped me nurture my dreams and turn them into lifelong past-times (and even careers!). I'm here because of you.

And finally, my deepest gratitude goes to you, dear reader. To the librarians and teachers and parents and kids (and every reader in between!), your kind letters and excitement have truly been life changing.

I'm so grateful you joined me for this latest ride . . . and can't wait for the next adventure.

ABOUT THE AUTHOR

K.R. Alexander is the pseudonym for author Alex R. Kahler.

As K.R., he writes thrilling, chilling books for adventurous young readers. As Alex—his actual first name—he writes fantasy novels for adults and teens. In both cases, he loves writing fiction drawn from true life experiences. (Though he has yet to visit a theme park where he could actually fly, his fingers are still crossed.)

Alex has traveled the world collecting strange and fascinating tales, from the misty moors of Scotland to the humid jungles of Hawaii. He is always on the move, as he believes there is much more to life than what meets the eye. As of this writing, Seattle is currently home.

K.R.'s other books include *The Collector, The Collected, The Fear Zone, The Fear Zone 2, The Undrowned, Vacancy,* and the books in the Scare Me series. You can contact him at cursedlibrary.com.

He looks forward to taking you on another wild ride very, very soon.

Read

K. R. Alexander...

if you dare

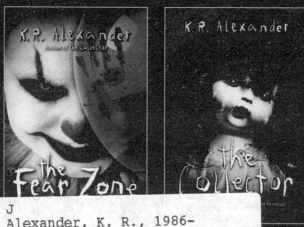

SCHOLASTIC
scholastic.com

ALEXANDER-COLLECTOR